Death Gets A Book

Frank J Edler

This book is dedicated to everyone
who has had to work an honest day's work
in their life.

Introduction

Did you come here looking for Death? I sure hope so! If you are one of the few people who has read my short story, DEATH GETS A LIFE, then *you* are the one responsible for this book! That's right, it's because of you and others like you that reached out to me and told me how much you were enamored with the character of Death in that story that I knew Death had more adventures to tell.

A lot of independent writers today have a signature series or character they hang their hat on. When I began venturing into writing, I never envisioned myself being that type of writer. I'm not into series or recurring characters all that much. But people kept coming to me asking if there was more Death stuff on the horizon. After being asked that enough I guess I came to the realization that there is something there that needs to be explored further. So I wrote another Death story, A DEATH IN TENNESSEE, to see if I could still write the character beyond that story. And I did, in a manner of speaking.

You see, Death isn't just one character (as anyone who has read DEATH GETS A LIFE) understands. In my world of Death, there are Deaths all over the world. Though humans may only recognize or think of Death as a single being, the reality is he can't really be in all those places all over the world at the same time, collecting up the souls whose time has come. It's kind of like the

Santa Clause thing, he's really got millions of helpers all over the world. And so it is with Deaths. There are thousands of them, all working their routes all over the world.

And it is with that idea in mind that I can tell the story of Death over and over again. Death is not one but many and each Death has a story to tell. So it is with this book that I tell another story of Death. This one a little longer and more epic than the others. And as a special treat to *you*, I've included the aforementioned short, A DEATH IN TENNESSEE in this volume as well.

Enjoy, and if there's a knock on the front door, be sure to finish reading this book before you answer it. It just may be Death knocking.

-Frank J Edler, October 2016

Prologue

Vincent walked the grimy streets of Tijuana searching for the head of a pink donkey with ridiculous bucked teeth. He wasn't having any luck. No luck at all.

Wanda swung her purse into the back of her husband Vincent's head. It was the third time she'd done it in the past half-hour. They were lost and he knew it. She knew it too and was in full bitch mode. She would nag and nag and nag until her seething boiled over and then *whack*!

"Ow, what the fuck, Wanda?!" Vincent shouted, rubbing the back of his head.

His wife could be such a bitch sometimes. All the time, now that he thought about it. His wife, Wanda, was an incessant nag. He was having a difficult time wondering why he brought her on his trip to Tijuana anyway. She was half the reason they were lost in a bad part of town, anyway.

The bickering couple wound their way through tight streets lined by cinder block houses. Vincent tried to keep a step or two ahead of his wife; the more he tried the more she tore into him for walking too fast.

"Do you think maybe you could at least walk with me?" his wife continued nagging.

"We're going to be late for the show!" Vincent insisted, keeping up his quickened pace.

"We're going to be dead if you don't get us out of this godforsaken place. This is not what I had in mind when you said we were going on vacation."

Vincent had said that he was going on vacation. She invited herself along. Just once, he would like to get away and be alone by himself. Away from her. Away from her nagging. Away from her bickering. But no, she insists on coming along wherever Vincent goes only to continue to bicker and nag and nag and nag.

Doesn't she get tired of it? Vincent knew he sure did. He was sick of it a long time ago. He often wondered why he put up with it. He felt trapped. His options outside of Wanda were limited at best. So he put up with the nagging all the time because if it wasn't Wanda it would be some other woman making his life miserable.

At least Wanda was willing to go to the Donkey show in Tijuana. There was that. Not many other women would allow their husband to go check out the infamous Tijuana Donkey show, let alone want to go see it as well. Vincent was certain that after it was over, Wanda would emerge from the show complaining about it the whole way back.

Vincent sighed as he looked for the marking on the building the seedy concierge back at the hotel told him to look for. It should stand out like a sore thumb. All the buildings in this run down barrio are nothing more than slate gray cinder block covered over with a minutia of junk for roofing. He'd been walking through these winding streets, some not much wider than a sidewalk in America, without seeing the elusive pink donkey painted over a concrete archway.

La Cantina Burro Rosa wasn't the most popular donkey show in Tijuana but it was supposed to be the most intense. It was the type of donkey show the locals would go see, not the watered down crap show they put on for the tourists downtown.

This was the real deal and it was the only reason Vincent was willing to brave the godforsaken streets of Tijuana and the relentless nagging from his wife.

"Vincent, my bunions are bursting. We need to stop. I need a drink of water, I'm thirsty. Why can't you just stop? I don't understand why we can't just turn around and go to a bar by the hotel?" Wanda sputtered out sounding like a human motor boat.

Vincent's nerves twitched. He knew she was winding up now to full on bitchery. The barrage of questions without leaving room for answers was one of the tell-tale signs. Soon the questions would be aimed at the buttons that make his psyche burst. After a few moments of those caliber questions coming at him, he would erupt and scream back, and World War MMXIII would be on. It was the same everyday and it always ended with the same question when he put his pounding head and frazzled nerves down to sleep: Why am I still married to this monster?

Before he could contemplate the existential thought any further, they reached an intersection where the tiny street opened up to a much wider thoroughfare. Vincent found what he was looking for. The pink donkey with the bucked teeth.

It was painted on the archway of a squat, white building. The arch was situated about eight feet in front of the building and rimmed with a short cinder block wall which created a small courtyard around the front of the otherwise nondescript building. There were no words, in Spanish or English, to indicate what type of business establishment this was. If not for the quirky pink donkey painted on the archway, there would have been no reason to believe this was any type of business at all.

"What a discovery, Ponce de Moron," Wanda said, shredding Vincent's nerves. "How about we quit staring at it and go inside so you can buy me something to drink. I'm ready to die of thirst from your sightseeing tour."

Vincent followed his wife in, a defeated man that knew he should feel triumphant in that moment.

***

The inside of the pink donkey club actually

looked like something. It was dimly lit but it had a sizable bar, a stage and a lot of cocktail tables scattered around the front of the stage. There was a peculiar musk to the air. Wanda chalked it up to the scent of third world Mexican body odor.

Wanda led her husband to a set of open bar stools. They both sat down and soaked in the ambiance. The place wasn't half as bad as Wanda was expecting it to be. She wasn't about to let her husband off the hook that easily though.

"Get me a zinfandel," she ordered Vincent.

"Hun, I don't think this is the type of bar that serves wine, sweetie," Vincent said meekly.

"What kind of bar doesn't serve wine? You dragged me through summer in Hell in the middle of a third world ghetto to a bar that doesn't serve wine? Vincent Mortimer Bennett, you get me a glass of wine or I am walking out of this bar and out of your life!"

The bartender was about to walk over to them but hesitated when Wanda raised her voice. Vincent hesitated. He hesitated a beat too long and Wanda pounced on him.

"Oh! What? That's what you want? You want me out of your life? Well, I've got news for you. You won't get rid of me that easily." She reached into her purse and pulled out a pack of cigarettes and a lighter.

She slid a cigarette out of the pack and lit it, her hands shaking like a Parkinson's patient the whole way. The tobacco glowed red at the end as she pulled a drag in long and deep. Then the tip erupted in a plume of smoke as her lungs eased off the nicotine fit. Her posture returned to a calm state.

The bartender approached them.

"¿Que quieres?" he asked.

"I'll have una cerveza, por favor," Vincent replied, trying to use as much Spanish as he knew, "and a zinfandel for my esposa."

The bartender tilted his head like a confused puppy, "¿Que? Zeen feen dell? No se, poppy."

Vincent turned to his wife, "He doesn't know what that is, hunny."

Wanda turned away from Vincent and leaned over the bar getting as close to the bartender's face as she could.

"I. Want-o. Pink-o. Zinfandel-a! Pronto!" she over enunciated.

Wanda wasn't going to put up with this shit. She knew damn well this bartender could speak English. And she knew this bar had to have pink zinfandel. What kind of bar didn't have pink zinfandel?

The bartender looked past Wanda, right at Vincent. His quick glare made it clear he was to calm his wife down or he was going to have a big problem.

"Vino! She would like vino. I'm sorry. Do

you have wine?" Vincent pleaded.

A light went on over the bartender's head. His threatening demeanor disappeared, replaced now by a big bright smile. He bent down behind the bar and popped back up a few moments later with a glass of wine. It was filled fuller than usual. It didn't appear to be a zinfandel; its hue was crimson not transparent pink.

Wanda was about to protest but her husband cut her off.

"Please dear, it's not what you want but it's a glass of wine and the bartender was gracious enough to overfill it for you. Please don't cause a scene here. This isn't the type of place to do that."

Wanda decided to end her protest. Not because her husband wanted her to, heaven knows she would never allow him that much space. She was pleased with the extra wine. She figured her show of force had earned her big glasses of wine for the evening, even if it wasn't the zinfandel she was accustomed to.

The bartender placed a bottle of beer in front of Vincent. It lacked a label identifying its brand but it was cold, dripping with sweat in the humid bar. Vincent looked pleased as punch to have a cold drink. That made Wanda irate.

Anything that made Vincent content made Wanda irate. She never considered why that was, it was just her natural reaction. Husbands should live to please their wives not themselves. That's how

Wanda saw things. She didn't give up on that principal, that is why she never grew tired of keeping Vincent in his place. It was all for his own good.

Wanda reached for her glass when the already scant lighting in the bar dimmed entirely. From the stage some overhead lights brightened. There must have been a piano down next to or behind the stage because some odd sounding ragtime music began to play.

A short, stocky Mexican gentleman dressed in a powdered blue tuxedo complete with white ruffles stolen from somewhere in 1955 entered from stage right. He walked up to the microphone at center stage, and the piano music stopped.

"Bienvenido a la Cantina Burro Rosa. El show de esta noche está a punto de comenzar. Por su propia seguridad, por favor no se acerque el escenario durante el espectáculo . Usted puede dejar una propina en el cubo en el camino de salida . Y ahora , te presentamos : Juan Arriba y el burro de color rosa!" the emcee in the blue tuxedo announced as he swept his hand toward the left of the stage.

Wanda leaned over to Vincent and asked, "Why do they have to speak Mexican wherever we go?"

Over the applause of the bar Vincent explained that they were speaking Spanish. Mexican isn't a language. Wanda was pissed at Vincent for trying to correct her. Of course they spoke Mexican in Mexico. She spoke American in America. Vincent was such an idiot. She would fix him yet.

***

Vincent tried as hard as he could to ignore his wife's flawed logic. When Juan took the stage followed close behind by his donkey, it became very easy to ignore her. The pink donkey sure lived up to its name. Kinda.

The donkey was indeed pink. It was obvious that pink wasn't the natural color of its coat. Vincent figured they most likely had cases of pink spray paint in the back because the donkey was still glistening with the fresh coat that appeared to be applied to it just before taking the stage. There were drips still running down its legs and sides from spots where they over sprayed.

La Cantina de Burro Rosa was intent on living up to its name: The Pink Donkey Bar.

Juan waved to the audience as they walked to center stage. The palm of his hand was as pink as his donkey.

He began talking (in Mexican, Vincent thought to himself as he rolled his eyes). Vincent had a rudimentary understand of Spanish but Juan spoke machine gun Spanish that his brain could not process. He decided to sit back and let the show speak for itself.

The ragtime piano began to play again. This time the tune was something a little sexier. It sounded like something from an 80s B-movie. Vincent knew them well. During his formative years he would stay up into the wee hours of the weekend waiting for the cheesy skin flicks to come on the premium cable channels. It was B-movies like that where Vincent first became aware of the world renowned Tijuana donkey shows.

Vincent was fifteen. The movie was called CrazyBalls 6. He had never watched CrazyBalls one through five, but had the distinct impression the plot lines of those weren't much different from part six. Like any great B-grade movie it started out with a buxom blonde naked as the day she was born. There were more college kids, jocks, nerds and vivacious vixens eager for a meager Hollywood paycheck than you could shake a stick at. CrazyBalls 6 was exactly like every other bad movie except it was every bad movie in Mexico.

No B-movie set in Mexico is ever complete without a reference to the Tijuana donkey shows. CrazyBalls 6 took it a little further than a reference and went so far as to actually have a scene inside one of the reclusive shows. The scene itself wasn't very detailed. Vincent was pretty sure the donkey was nothing more that stock footage from an old nature documentary interspersed with poorly edited close-ups of one of the supporting actresses. But if a young teenaged mind was allowed to imagine the possibilities, the blanks could easily be filled in to your liking.

When CrazyBalls 6 had ended around two a.m. on that fateful Sunday morning, Vincent knew it was his life's quest to go see one of the Tijuana donkey shows for himself. That was why, at the age of fifty-seven, he sat here in this dingy bar in one of the most run-down areas of the world preparing to watch whatever it was that happens during one of these shows. The fact was, Vincent didn't know what happened for sure, he hoped it lived up to the idea he had built up in his mind when he was fifteen years old.

Next to him, Wanda picked up her glass of wine. Vincent reached over and placed his hand over her forearm, stopping her from taking a sip. He spotted an open cocktail table up front by the stage. He told Wanda to take her drink and follow him.

They got up from the bar and worked their way over to the cocktail table, A few of the men in attendance voiced their disapproval of the two interrupting the show. Vincent shrugged, trying to plead stupid American. Wanda gave them the finger.

They sat down. They were so close to the stage they could smell the animal musk mingled with pink spray paint. Wanda kicked Vincent in the shin under the table trying to start another argument. Vincent was not going to be swayed this time. He was front row for the donkey show. He found his happy place.

***

What the fuck is wrong with him? Wanda thought to herself.

She nailed him with the pointed tip of her shoe right in the shin and he didn't even flinch. She was embarrassed that Vincent made them get up and walk in front of everyone while they were trying to watch this perverted show. He didn't peel his eyes off the stage, and he was smiling like he never smiled at her. This was war.

Before she could continue bringing her husband back down to Earth, something on stage also grabbed her attention.

Juan flung his long bathrobe off. He was dressed in leather. Only, it was a leather bikini. Well, the bottoms were a bikini, and the top was two leather pasties complete with black leather tassels affixed upon his nipples. The crowd in the bar went crazy. Wanda's eyes widened to the size of dinner plates.

She wasn't sure what she was expecting to see at the donkey show. She was just going along with her husband. She wasn't going to let him out of her sight in Mexico, and she wanted to see the town herself. In the moment that she watched leather tasseled Juan spin his nipple tassels to and fro as he walked around to the ass side of his pink ass, too many truths became evident.

First, this donkey was about to do something

nature never intended it to do. Second, Juan was a sick fuck. And finally, why in the name of all things holy did her husband purposely come here to see this show and then take front row where he forgot that the rest of the world existed?

Wanda, having a sensory overload, grabbed her wine and threw back the entire glass. That's when things got even worse.

***

Vincent was hard as a rock. A lifetime of repressed sexual excitement culminated to this moment. His heart was pumping like it had not done so in the past thirty years. He watched as Juan did a seductive dance for his donkey counterpart. Vincent fought the urge to jump on stage and join Juan; there was more than enough ass up there for two guys to handle.

His trance was broken when a cloud of crimson mist doused the side of the pink donkey. Vincent thought someone had shot it at first but there was no loud crack from a gun. He looked at his wife, stunned, unsure of what just happened.

Wanda's mouth looked as if she had just performed the blood spitting routine at a *Kiss* concert. Thick red mucus dripped from around her mouth down onto her blouse. She looked like she was ready to vomit.

Vincent's mind could not process what was

happening. "What the hell?" he whimpered as his boner slumped back down to where it had been for the past two decades.

From behind them the bartender was laughing out loud and pointing at Wanda. He kept saying, "Sangre! Sangre!" to the others in the bar who were also confused as to what just happened. The others in the bar began to laugh as well at the explanation.

Vincent, who also understood "sangre", didn't laugh. He became mortified. Sangre was Spanish for blood. He served Wanda a glass of blood to fuck with her for being a bitch. He wanted to admire the bartender for paying back the bitch but he knew a shit storm was about to blow over La Cantina de Burro Rosa.

Wanda stood up in front of the stage. She turned around, trembling with hate. She screeched like an owl, "WHAT THE FUCK IS SO FUCKING FUNNY!?"

The sudden shrill explosion of anger and hate from his wife's mouth must have scared the pink donkey because all of a sudden Vincent watched his wife's head explode like a pumpkin as the donkey back-kicked her cranium with both its hind quarters.

Before Vincent could appreciate his bachelorhood, the donkey kicked again and obliterated Vincent's skull as well.

Chapter One: A Death in Tijuana

Death woke up in Mexico with a pounding headache.

It must be Tuesday, Death thought to himself as he shielded the glare of the sun with the sleeve of his black, tattered robe. "Or Wednesday or Thursday or any of the other days ending in day."

Death picked his weary bones up off the decrepit back alley. He had passed out behind a dumpster behind some craggy restaurant by the smell of things. A thick, pungent, rotting musk filled the air. Death realized he may have been the source of the odor and not the dumpster. Such was life for Death.

He achieved a more or less upright posture as his head swooned and his brain began to pound. This was odd, seeing as to the best of his knowledge, he had no brain. Not a physical one anyway.

Death was all bones. He looked like a skeleton from fifth grade science class minus the pesky metal stand to hold him up. He was also much more animated that that unfortunate plastic model. Though his face was all bone, the bone could still articulate facial expressions and the like. And of course, the whole affair was covered over discretely by the standard issue Black Tattered Robe™ as issued by the League of Deaths (Greater Oaxacan Division).

When the cobwebs cleared from his head he searched around. He was looking for the only other standard issue piece from the League: his scythe. The scythe was an important part of the Death uniform. Death had no idea why, but it was beaten into him during training that the scythe was never to leave his side. It was like a soldier's rifle or Indiana Jones' fedora - you just didn't ever lose it or you would be sorry.

"Ah ha!" he said spying its handle poking out from the dumpster and grabbing it. "That would have sucked."

He brushed some trash off his Black Tattered Robe™ thinking it may have been better to leave it on. The grimy look always helped with the Death appearance. Still, he knew he only gets one Black Tattered Robe™ during his tenure at The League so he figured he should at least try to keep it as nice as possible for as long as he could.

The more he moved around, the more his skull pounded. Who knew Deaths were prone to hangovers? That's something they never cover in training. He tried to reign in his faculties enough to figure out what he was going to do. He had to get back to the office in time to get his daily assignment.

He grasped the sides of his skull with his skeletal hands, trying to ease the drum beat in his head. Could Death call out of work? Was that a thing? If it was he needed to do so, pronto. How would he even call out? Death wasn't issued a cell phone. He was going to have to go in. The light of day was already cutting down into the shadows of the alley. He was going to be late, of that he was certain.

A screeching voice cut through the air, "Death! Death? Where are you!" It was shrill like a voice made entirely of Jimi Hendrix's amplifier feedback.

Death's hand vibrated with each word. He fought back the splitting pain in his head and looked at his hand where the vibration was coming from. It was the hand holding his scythe.

"Death! We have an emergency assignment!"

He followed the wooden handle of the scythe to the nasty curved metal blade at the end. Death could see it vibrating in time with the voice tearing through the air. What the hell?

"I... I'm here?" he replied to the disembodied voice.

"Why are you in an alley and not in the office? We've got a hot one, close to your position. Two unexpecteds. Pick them up and I'll ignore your tardiness this morning. The Pink Donkey, just down the street from your current position. Get 'em. Now!"

"Shit." Death said.

Death crawled out of the gutter and into the streets of Tijuana.

***

Tiburcio blotted the sweat from his bulbous forehead. He was still dressed in his powdered blue tuxedo. There was no time to change out of it, he had to clean up the mess the two Americanos caused. He cursed them under the early morning sun that beat down on the barren slope just behind La Cantina Burro Rosa, the bar that his family had been operating since the early 1900's.

"Hernando! Juan! Dig faster. I want this done before the policia get here." he commanded the two men digging.

Whenever Americans went missing, the police were sure to show. Tiburcio had been there before. La Cantina Burro Rosa was meant for locals. The Americans were supposed to stay downtown where all the stuff there was built for them and taking their dollars. It never failed though, from time to time stupid Americans would wander into his cantina looking for an authentic donkey show.

They would find it, too. La Cantina Burro Rosa put on the most authentic Tijuana donkey show there was. Tiburcio's family invented the very concept. His great great abuela, Jaunita and her donkey Felipe were the first to take the stage at the cantina. Her donkey was pink tinged from being coated in the dust from the dry dust that was always kicked up around the foothills behind the bar. The show was an instant hit, spawned urban legend and the bar was named to honor his great great grandmother's donkey, The Pink Donkey, Felipe.

Not long after, the downtown area was bustling with bars putting on donkey shows. The Americans ate it up. But those shows were all watered down nonsense. The locals knew they had to come to La Cantina Burro Rosa for the authentic experience. Nothing had ever been held back. Eventually, an American would get wind of the place and brave the dangerous barrio streets to watch the urban legend for themselves. But it always came at a price.

That was how Vincent and Wanda Bennett found themselves with pulverized heads, inside worn out burlap sacks, dead as the scrub brush they were about to be buried amongst.

"Come on faster, Hernando!" Tiburcio yelled.

"I'm going as fast as I can boss." Hernando called back, winded.

"If you hadn't given the gringos the blood of the bull to drink you wouldn't be in this situation. This is a lesson for your pranks."

"Ahh, the gringa, she had it coming to her. I was doing her husband a favor."

"Is that so Hernando? I am sure he is thanking you from inside that burlap bag."

Hernando shrugged and smiled. He got back to digging.

"And you, Juan. Why did you use so much paint on Lolita." He motioned to the donkey, still dripping pink spray paint from her coat, grazing from her bucket of feed. "You know she gets irritated when you use too much."

"Si, jeffe. I know. But my girl, Flora, she was there last night. I wanted Lolita to look her best for the performance. Flora thought she looked just beautiful. She did, don't you think?"

Tiburcio threw his hands to the air. "Idiotas!" he cried out. "That's it, stop digging. That is deep enough; we don't have time for this. Put the bodies in and and let's finish up."

"But boss," Hernando said, "the hole is not deep enough at all. The dogs will be digging at the graves by nightfall."

"By nightfall the policia will have come and gone. Then it is no longer our problem. Put them in, let's go!"

Juan and Hernando tossed the bodies into their respective holes. The graves were just deep enough to fit the bodies below ground level. However, when they filled the shallow graves back over, the dirt mounded high above the surface.

Tiburcio was satisfied the dead scrub brush and general rolling topography of the slope would hide the graves enough. The policia would come, but their investigation would only be cursory, just enough to satisfy the American authorities that they had tried.

Tiburcio recalled Juan and Hernando back inside the bar. The mess was cleaned up. It was time to get ready for another night at La Cantina Burro Rosa.

***

Death made his way out of the Zona Norte section of Tijuana and onto the bustling Avenida Revolucion. He wasn't worried about the bevy of activity going on around him; people just didn't see death unless Death came for them. It was one of the perks of the job.

Death hurried down the sidewalk, weaving around people who could not see him. All of a sudden a little boy no more than eight years old jumped out in front of him. The boy pointed at Death, laughing. Death, not expecting the kid to jump in his path stumbled over the kid like he was a dog that got under his feet. They both flopped on to the ground.

Death lingered down on his back, trying to recuperate from the fall. The kid was right up on his feet, full of vigor. He stood over Death and pointed at him again.

"Ha! Ha! You look like an idiota!" he said in a mocking, sing-song tone.

Death look at the kid, confused. "What? You can see me?"

"I see you, idota! You look like a girl!" he

giggled as he spoke.

"Boy, if you see me, you better get home to your mama quick so she can say goodbye."

"I'm not scared of you. You look like a clown!"

Death sat up. He looked around for some sort of mirror to look in. What in Hades' name was this kid talking about?

A Volkswagen Beetle rolled up and stopped near the curb where Death was lying on the sidewalk. He looked into the rounded, polished metal hub cap. He gasped at the grotesque image that stared back at him. His face was elongated and twisted in the curves and dings of the hubcap, but that wasn't what disturbed him. His face was painted like a colorful skull mask popular during the Mexican Dia de los Muertos. The Day of the Dead.

Someone must have happened upon him while he was passed out in the alley and painted his face like a sugar skull. They must have been able to work fast seeing as his face already had the skull features built in. His black, hollow eye sockets were ringed with pink semicircles, like tiny flower petals. His cheekbones were painted on with yellow paisley like squiggles. There was a pink web design on his forehead and a pink rose painted on the front of his lower jaw bone.

Whoever did it didn't even do a good job. It looked like the work of a kindergartener or worse yet, a drunk. The kid was right, he did look like an idiota.

He broke his trance staring at himself in the dinged up hubcap of the Punch Buggy. He noted its color, red, and went to punch the kid in the arm. "Punch Buggy red!" Death said, cocking his fist back. But the kid was gone; he had taken off.

Death got up off the ground for the second time that morning. He brushed himself off and composed himself once more. His scythe rattled violently on the ground as the mysterious voice erupted from it once more.

"Death! Death! Quit screwing around or you're going to lose your charges!" it boomed in its high pitched screech. The voice had all the impatience of a metropolitan newspaper editor with a deadline looming.

Death grabbed his scythe. He decided waking was the wrong approach. He took a look around and when he was satisfied nobody else around him could see him like the kid did, he dematerialized.

***

Death rose from the grave. He had a vague idea of who he was. He had a vague idea he was something else not long ago. The feeling ran from his mind like a fleeting idea.

He was naked. Naked inasmuch as he was a living skeleton, not a stitch of clothing on him. He was not ashamed of his natural form. He made no effort to cover up. Instead he reached his bony arms to the sky and stretched out as if he had been cooped up in the shallow grave beneath him for a millennia. In fact, he was only there for mere seconds.

I am Death, he thought to himself, like a voice in his head that was his but independent of his own mind.

Death materialized in front of Death.

"Shit," the new Death on the scene said.

The new Death looked at the materialized Death. "You look like an idiot."

If materialized Death had eyes in his hollow, black sockets, he would have rolled them. "Yes, yes I know. But we have bigger concerns than my bad make-up job right now."

"Meaning what?"

"Meaning you are Death and I'm in deep shit."

"I knew I was Death, somehow. Did you make me this way? Is that why you're in deep shit?"

"Well, I did and I didn't. I didn't make you Death. Not directly. But I did get drunk, pass out in a seedy alley in Tijuana and get my face painted like a sugar skull by a bunch of derelict toddlers. And that led to you being Death."

"I don't follow."

"Look, not more than a few hours ago you were known as Vincent Bennett. You were a human from Chattanooga, Tennessee. You were on vacation with your wife, Wanda." He motioned to the shallow grave in juxtaposition to the one underneath Death's feet. "When you both got yourselves killed in that bar down the hill behind you."

Death looked over his shoulder at the bar and then back to Death. He wasn't following, none of it made sense.

"I was supposed to lead you and your wife's souls across the Styx and to the Hereafter. But, I had a rough morning and didn't make it in time. The unexpected calls are a bitch. Anyway, your soul was buried and... Voila! You are now a Death. Like me. Like all the others."

"There are more like us?"

"Thousands. I ain't Santa Claus, pal. I can't get it all done in one night. It takes an army to lead that many souls to the Hereafter. Over one hundred and fifty thousand a day. That's why we spread out. Handle the calls regionally. It's not the perfect system but it gets the job done."

"So, what's your name anyway?" the Death formerly known as Vincent asked.

"Name? I don't have a name. We don't have names. We are Death," Death answered.

"So when I call you and you're standing around with all your other Death buddies, you're all going to turn and look at me and not know which one of you I'm talking to? That doesn't make any sense."

The ground next to them began to rumble. The loose dirt over Wanda's shallow grave began to crumble away from the center. Clumps of dirt pushed upward. She was rising. There was a small pocket deep down somewhere in a part of Death's psyche that still clung onto a piece of who Vincent was and when that piece realized his wife was coming back, all of Death became crestfallen.

Before Death had an opportunity to be retaken by that depression, Death collared him around the neck bone and scurried away from the grave site. They ran down the slope to the back of the pink building that sat at the foot of the hill. Death and Death took cover behind a collection of fly infested garbage cans.

They got there just in the nick of time. Wanda's grave exploded in a plume of dirt. A black figure, the blackest black that could be fathomed, shot out of the hole like a cannon ball and zipped up into the sky. A loud, sad wailing, like a depressed fire engine emanated from the figure as it shot off toward the horizon.

"What the hell was that?" the Death formerly known as Vincent asked.

"Your wife," the Death from Tijuana replied.

Chapter Two: Death Gets a Book

Death knew he should be scared. He wasn't sure why. Should he be scared of his wife? Or should he be scared that that thing was his wife? Neither option was good and he only had fleeting feelings as to why he should be worried in the first place. Trying to grasp his emotions was like trying to catch a soap bubble, every time you got close, it vanished into thin air.

"You need to get the book," the Death from Tijuana told him, still casting a cautious glance out of the horizon line where the black figure had gone.

"What book?" the Death formerly known as Vincent asked.

"You need to get to a field office. They will give you the book. And the robe, the scythe, an assignment, the whole nine. I don't know if you've noticed but you're naked right now, and your impressive hip bones are making me a bit jealous." Death indicated his own narrow gauge hips underneath his Black Tattered Robe™. "So just go to the office and get outfitted and stuff and you'll be all set."

Vincent Death freaked out. "I don't know where the office is! I don't know what this book is you're talking about! I don't know a thing about

Deathing! And I have no idea why you have pelvis envy! As a matter of fact, it occurs to me that you, by your own admission, are responsible for the way I am right now so I think you owe it to me to escort me to the office and show me the ropes. Get me a damned clue as to what the fuck is going on here exactly!"

The Death from Tijuana had taken a step back during Death's tirade. He'd been a Death for eons now, maybe longer. He forgot what it was like for him when he first became Death. He also realized he had to get back to the office himself. He had yet to receive his assignments for the day after having woken up in a drunken haze and then being called out here on an emergency pick-up. He supposed getting this Death on the right foot would be the least he could do for the guy.

"Look, uhhh, I'm sorry. I have to get back to the office myself so why don't you come with me and I'll introduce you to all the right people. Get you set up. Get you started on the right foot."

Vincent Death considered the offer but not for long. "That sounds alright. I guess I'm stuck like this so I may as well."

"That's the spirit! C'mon, I'll show you the first cool thing we can do. Grab my bone."

Death looked at Death. He didn't realize it was that kind of a deal. He flinched back.

"No, you nincompoop! Look, the sexual innuendo is out the window now. That's for the flesh wearers, the only bones we've got are the ones that crumble." He grabbed Death's bony arm and they vaporized out of sight.

***

Death sat at a tattered wooden desk, almost hidden by stacks of overstuffed manila envelopes. He clamped the cigarette between his teeth and drew deep. The embers glowed cherry red before expelling thick gray smoke. He was cursing a steady stream of obscenities. The mood was punctuated by poor fluorescent lighting, the kind that strobes just enough to drive you mad.

Vincent Death wasn't comfortable approaching this Death at all. The Death from Tijuana urged him forward, closer to the Death behind the desk. The cursing Death was so embroiled in his own paper fueled madness he never noticed them approach until the Death from Tijuana cleared his throat.

"Excuse me. Sir?"

"Gah!" Paperwork exploded all over the place as the Death behind the desk jumped from the sudden, unexpected interruption. "What the fucking fuck are you fucking sneaking the fuck up on me like that for, you putrid piece of shit?! Who the fuck is this and why are you not out doing your poor excuse of a job? Shit! They may as well walk into this office and shit on my desk." He hammered his skeletal fist on the only bare spot causing a loud bang that made the other two Deaths jump themselves. "They may as well walk into this office, stand on this desk and take a crap right on it and tell me that's my new employee. It would make a hell of a lot more sense and I'm sure that pile of crap wouldn't have to be roused the fuck up on a Tuesday morning in some God forsaken alley in a town the Devil himself wouldn't be caught dead in. You're a piece of shit, you know that Death?"

The Death from Tijuana looked down to the floor, hiding his head as far between his shoulder blades as possible. "Yes, sir. The biggest piece of shit sir."

"And you brought your little turdlette with you too?" the Death behind the desk asked, eyeing Vincent Death up and down like he was just that, an afterthought pebble of a turd after the main log had been discharged.

"Yes sir. This is—" the Death from Tijuana paused, trying to find the right words. There were none. "This is my fuck up, sir."

The Death behind the desk flicked his half smoked cigarette at the Death from Tijuana. "So, you didn't make it, you drunken slob. If you weren't already dead, I'd kill you. You understand that, don't you? I don't need any more Death around here, I'm neck deep in you fuck-ups already."

Vincent Death felt like prey that was being played with just before it was devoured. He was not liking this Death business at all. He walked in this office feeling contempt for the Death from

Tijuana for putting him in this predicament. Now he felt awful for him. He imagined this is how it was for him, day in and day out.

The Death behind the desk slid open a drawer behind his desk. He fished out a set of keys. They jingled like bells on a sleigh. The key ring was loaded with keys. It was also loaded with other key rings that were also loaded with other keys and key rings. It was a giant brass ball of keys. The Death behind the desk threw the keys like a softball at the Death from Tijuana.

The Death from Tijuana wasn't able to react fast enough and the ball of keys nailed him right in the chest. Vincent Death heard something snap, a rib he guessed. The ball of keys clanked to the floor. The Death from Tijuana rubbed his chest then used his scythe to hook the keys up off the floor. He righted his scythe at his side, the keys dangling from the blade like a Christmas ornament.

"Take your turdlette down to Resources. Get him outfitted. I'm going to make a call down there, get him assigned somewhere else. Let someone else wipe this shit up, I'm all outta paper. Get the fuck out of my sight. Both of you!"

The Death behind the desk disappeared behind the mountain of paperwork once again. Vincent Death heard the snap/zip of a cigarette lighter and smoke soon billowed up from behind the manila forest. The stream of obscenities once again began to flow in earnest.

"C'mon," the Death from Tijuana said, "let's get you outfitted."

"That guy is an asshole," Vincent Death said after they cleared the office.

"He's a supervisor," the Death from Tijuana responded, still keeping his voice down even out of earshot, "they are all the same."

***

They walked down the hall from the supervisor's office. The hall was long and narrow and lit with the same drab fluorescent lighting like in the office. Every twenty feet or so the hall was broken by a small recess and a door. First to the left then twenty feet then a door to the right. One door looked the same as the other and the only thing to differentiate them was what side of the hall they were at.

To Vincent Death, it felt like they had walked a mile and made no progress forward. Just when he thought walking the infinite hallway was going to be how he spent the rest of his life as Death, the Death from Tijuana stopped and opened a door on the right. Vincent Death had no idea how he knew that was the door they were looking for, for it was unmarked and plain, indistinguishable from the others.

They stepped through the door and found the inside was anything but ordinary. Vincent Death wondered how the hallway outside was so silent and still with the bevy of activity and noise that was taking place just inside the door. The door opened into a large warehouse. The warehouse seemed to go as far as they had walked in all directions. Vincent Death wondered why they didn't just go in the first door on the right that they came to. The warehouse was so humongous it had to envelope every door on the right that they passed.

"How come we didn't just walk in the first door on the right?" Vincent Death asked.

"Because that was processing. We don't want processing. We want outfitting," the Death from Tijuana replied as if he were being hounded with questions from a curious five-year-old.

"This warehouse is so big it must span back to that first door," Vincent Death insisted.

"Death," the Death from Tijuana said trying to maintain his patience, "there must have been a hundred doors between there and here. That's a hundred different rooms. Those are those rooms and this door leads to this room. Why can you not understand that?"

Vincent Death chose not to pursue his line of questioning with physical reasoning. It was apparent that a lot of the rules no longer applied and he was going to have to start getting used to that if he was going to have a successful new career.

"Darlings!" squawked a high pitched, flamboyant voice.

Vincent Death looked to the source of the voice. Death approached them. This Death didn't walk over to them so much as it glided toward them, with a grand flair for the dramatic as well. The flamboyant Death was dressed in the signature Tattered Black Robe™ but the robe portion at the bottom was more form fitting, like a dress. It was also hemmed up much higher than the standard ground length robes he had seen. The flamboyant Death wore his robe cut at knee level, and spoke in a sing-songy voice.

"Hello! How can I help you gentlemen today?"

Before either of them had a moment to answer, the flamboyant Death made a ghastly realization and gasped, inhaling in a high pitch, "Darling! You have no clothes on!"

Vincent suddenly felt like the flamboyant Death was eyeing him up like his next meal. The kind of meal you have rough sex with before you devour it.

"Oh my! Impressive hipbone," the flamboyant Death said with a wink of his hollow black eye socket.

The Death from Tijuana cut in, trying to get back to business, "Boss says we need to get this one outfitted right away. Full standard issue."

The flamboyant Death looked at the Death from Tijuana with contempt. He was annoyed he had to get back to work when he was having so much fun being playful with the new guy. The subtle machinations were lost on Vincent Death, there was too much new stuff to take in. He just went with the program.

The flamboyant Death led them down one of the endless aisles in the warehouse, gliding along like a movie star in the process. Vincent Death and the Death from Tijuana followed close behind examining the contents of the high shelves as they walked past. A carton of spare scythe blades here, a shrink-wrapped pallet marked 'Soul Jars' and an unopened, dust covered box labeled 'Tattered Black Robe™ patches'.

They reached the end of a row of shelving which opened up into an area with a row of office cubicles. Vincent Death was ushered into the cubicle on the far right. The cubicle wall came up to about his shoulders, still exposing his head.

The flamboyant Death reached over the cubicle and handed Vincent Death a folded up Tattered Black Robe™.

"Here," the flamboyant Death said, "standard issue. You may not alter, modify or otherwise change it in any way, shape or form. It is the only one you will receive while you are in service to The League. Now try it on."

Vincent Death grabbed the garment and let it unfold. It was black, the blackest of black. It was heavy and woolen. It felt scratchy, like a burlap sack. The robe wasn't musty or dusty like he would have expected but it didn't have a new clothes smell to it either. The more he examined it, the more he found it a breathtaking piece of clothing.

"Why am I in a changing cubicle," Vincent began as he maneuvered the Tattered Black Robe™ over his head, "when I've been walked around bone naked the whole time without any issues?"

"League regulations," the flamboyant Death said. "Believe me I'm no happier about it than you are." He gave Vincent Death another wink.

"What is this League you keep talking about?" Vincent Death asked.

"The League of Deaths," the Death from Tijuana replied, "is the collective organization of Deaths all around the world. The League is broken up into regional field offices. You are in the Greater Oxocan Field Office. It doesn't matter where you are inducted, in the end, you work for The League. They own you now."

"Step out." the flamboyant Death instructed.

Vincent Death stepped out of the cubicle. The Tattered Black Robe™ fit him to a tee; he was the very model image of Death. He felt good being in it. The weight of it draped around his shoulder felt natural, he felt a power just wearing it.

"Pull the hood over your skull. You are never to appear among any of your charges without the hood over your head. There are severe repercussions for violating that rule," the flamboyant Death told him.

Vincent Death pulled the hood on over his head. His skull was shrouded in darkness. In Vincent Death's mind, ominous music started to play. He felt sparks coursing through his bones, like a switch was turned on and shot current through his skeletal remains. It felt incredible. He was Death.

"Okay flyboy, quit beaming with pride. You're not fully outfitted yet," the flamboyant Death said. "There are still a few more things. Follow me this way."

The flamboyant Death glided down one of the endless aisles in the warehouse. Vincent Death and the Death from Tijuana glided after him. Vincent Death felt like he was gliding along now with the robe on. It was as if his feet never touched the ground but padded along on a small cushion of air. It was an odd yet liberating feeling.

The aisle they moved along stopped at a dead end. Against the wall was a caged cabinet. The flamboyant Death fished around in his robe and produced a key. He unlocked the cage which revealed a large collection of identical scythes. They weren't remarkable looking. None of the blades shined like newly polished metal. The handles were painted a dull gunmetal black. The only thing impressive was the sheer amount of them piled into the locker.

Still, the flamboyant Death eyed them up as if he were looking for one in particular. He shot a glance at Vincent Death looking up and down then continued analyzing the locker full of scythes. He reached in, shuffling a few out of the way digging toward one a few layers deeper within.

The flamboyant Death pulled a scythe he seemed to pick specifically among the seemingly identical collection and presented it to Vincent Death. "Here, this one has your name on it."

Vincent Death took hold of it, bewildered. "They all look exactly alike. How do you know this is the perfect one for me? There is nothing to differentiate them from one another."

"I just told you, it has your name on it."

Vincent Death examined it. Inscribed on the handle, right about where he would place his hand on the shaft, the name 'DEATH' was inscribed into the dark wood. "But, we're all named Death," Vincent said, confused.

"How convenient," the flamboyant Death replied, unamused. "You'll never forget who you are now. This way!"

The flamboyant Death whisked off back up the aisle. The Death from Tijuana clanged scythe blades with Vincent Death like he was toasting to his new life and followed after the other Death. Vincent shook his head. He didn't expect this whole outfitting business to be such an adventure in and of itself. He hurried after the other two before they were out of sight.

***

Vincent Death moved fast, trying to keep up with the other two. There were turns up and down the aisles so fast he was becoming disoriented. He felt like a mouse running through a maze. The two Deaths ahead of him made a series of quick maneuvers around tight turns. Vincent Death had lost sight of them.

He panicked. This warehouse was so vast, he doubted he would ever be able to find his way out even if he had a millennium to do so. He guessed at the direction they went, taking a quick left and then two rights around a dizzying array of aisles. He had no idea where he was going yet he almost felt like he was being guided. Then he noticed it was his hand holding the scythe that seemed to be leading the way like he was holding a divining rod and it was pulling him every so slightly in a particular direction.

Just as he became mesmerized by the sensation, he took another turn and found the two Deaths standing in a clearing among the aisles. They had their arms folded, impatient.

"Hey, is this thing like a homing device? Vincent asked as he glided up to them. "I felt like it was leading me to you two."

"Its many things. Don't ever lose that," was all the flamboyant Death gave him for an answer.

"Yeah, mine was yelling at me this morning before I, uhh, came to get you," the Death from

Tijuana said trying to make a joke.

Vincent Death didn't laugh.

"This is our library. There is only one book contained within it. It is the only book you will ever need and it contains everything you need to know within it. Once you have the book you will report to dispatch for your orders."

Vincent Death looked around. "I don't see any library or books." He spun around looking only at aisles and aisles of tall metal shelving.

The flamboyant Death tapped the handle of his scythe on the floor twice. It made a hollow knocking noise. Vincent Death looked to the ground where he rapped the scythe. There was an old, cracked wooden door in the floor. The Death from Tijuana hooked the blade of his scythe around the brass ring that served as a knob and pulled it open. It swung open with a loud, reverberating creak as a plume of dust erupted from the black hole in the floor.

"This way," the flamboyant Death said and hovered over the hole, levitating down like he rode an invisible elevator. The Death from Tijuana did the same. Vincent Death took a leap of faith figuring if he could glide he could float. He stepped over the abyss ready to hover but instead fell straight down into the hole.

Fortune fell on him as he fell on top of the Death from Tijuana who was still levitating down into the library. They fell the last few feet and tumbled onto the ground.

"Are you crazy?" the Death from Tijuana yelled at him, pushing him off.

"You don't have the book yet. What gave you the idea you could levitate? I just told you that book contains everything you will need to know and you don't know levitating because you don't have the book. This isn't so hard a concept to grasp, is it?"

"I... it's just, I thought... with the gliding... and you both... ahhh... Sorry?" Vincent Death mumbled.

"Don't ever think you can do anything without consulting the book first," the flamboyant Death admonished with the tone of a grade school teacher. "The book contains all the rules. Every policy and procedure. The do's and the don'ts. Follow the book and you will have a successful career at The League. Break the rules and you will find out there are worse fates than death."

The flamboyant Death handed the book over to Vincent Death. He took the book and tucked it away inside his Tattered Black Robe™. He found a fold within the robe and was surprised to find the weight of the book did not translate to added weight on the robe. It was as if disappeared within the confines of the Tattered Black Robe™. He reached for it to be sure it was still there and as he grasped its thick spine, he felt the weight of it again.

"Hey that's pretty cool!" Vincent Death mused.

"It's in the book," grumbled the flamboyant Death. "Now, get out of here and go get your assignment."

The flamboyant Death rose up and out of the pit.

"Well, one last stop and then I've done my duty," the Death from Tijuana said. "The assignment desk isn't that far a walk from here but let me show you something cool. I'm going to grab your shoulder and you're going to take us right there. Ready?"

"Ahh, yeah. Hang on let me look up how to do this in the book," Vincent Death said.

"Pfft. The book? You don't need that book, put it away. I'll just tell you how it's done, it's pretty easy. I know that guy went on and on about the book but really, a lot of it is just common sense and you know yourself a lot of it just comes natural. Like the book pocket in the robe, you didn't know it was there but you grabbed the book and tucked it in there without a second thought. There is a lot of instinct when you're a Death. You'll see."

"Now," the Death from Tijuana grabbed Vincent Death's shoulder, "let's blow this grave and get you to work."

Vincent Death just stood there. He wasn't sure what he was supposed to do. Nothing was coming to him naturally.

Chapter 3: Another Death in Tennessee

Wanda was consumed with misery. She felt guilt and grief. She felt deep a deep sadness. She felt cold, dark despair. She felt trapped.

She *was* trapped. It was someplace dank and dark and claustrophobic. Pressure closed in on her from all sides. The more she struggled, the greater the force pushed on her whole body. This fed her misery.

She was weakened but felt herself becoming stronger. She felt like herself but something different, someone new. She felt like she was being reborn within a womb. That made her mournful.

All her emotions, all this dirt she felt encased in collapsed her soul to an infinite point of anger. That mass of emotion exploded out of her like a cataclysmic cosmic event. She erupted from the Earth that enslaved her. She ran from there as fast as she could, away from all those terrible, awful emotions that had overcome her, eating away at her soul like battery acid. She ran faster than she could ever remember, crying so hard she was wailing. Yet, as fast as she ran from there, the anguish that enveloped her was not left behind.

After some time, she realized the melancholy was a part of her now. It was overwhelming but she was becoming numb to it after the initial shock. She slowed down. By the time she stopped, she realized she was back home in Memphis, Tennessee. She'd gone a long way in a short time.

The sadness was now a monkey on her back. She couldn't shake it. She resigned herself to it; it was a part of her now. She just wanted to go home. She ambled her way there, people she passed on the streets ignored her as if she wasn't there at all. Who could blame them? Nobody is comfortable around those who are grief stricken. Wanda felt like the most grief struck person on Earth at the moment and she had no idea why.

She opened the door to her house. It was quiet, too quiet. Something was missing. She looked around. Everything felt out of place, nothing felt homey about the house. She grew frantic searching for something that could root her back home. The anguish boiled up within her in her frenzy. She ran to the mantle in the living room, crashing head first into a menagerie of framed photographs lined up on the ledge. Glass shattered and pictures crashed all around her. She lifted her head, tears streaming down her eyes again, and looked at the picture she destroyed with her head.

Through a prism of shattered glass she found what was missing. Her husband, Vincent. He was not here; he was gone. Her sadness mutated to rage. Vincent was gone. Vincent was not here; he left her. That son of a bitch had left her. He would pay; she would not stand for it. Vincent could never leave her.

Whatever remained of the person once known as Wanda Benedict left her at that moment. She cried with rage. It disturbed and frightened her until the last bits of her soul vanished. Then the hateful cry comforted her. It was a pressure valve. She wailed at the mantel of the house that she no longer called home until the raw ball of negative emotions that drove her reached a controllable level.

Now she had to find Vincent. How was she going to find Vincent?

***

Aileen and Maggie O'Kelly were clearing off the dinner table. It was a typical evening for Aileen. She was trying to navigate her mid-life crisis not only in a new home but in a new country. She thought she had left Ireland to escape her problems but her mother, Maggie, would hound her like clockwork as they finished up dinner about finding a man and settling down. It was times like that that she felt her sainted mother was the source of her woes.

"Aileen O'Kelly, won't you go out tomorrow night and find yourself a husband instead of staying home again tending to me?" her mother would ask.

"Mom, I can't just leave you here alone. You

don't have strength enough to cook for yourself or get yourself up to visit the loo or get to bed," Aileen tried to reason with her.

Maggie was no spring chicken. She could still get along but she needed a lot of help. She couldn't live alone any longer but Aileen wouldn't dream of putting her in a home. Aileen didn't have to work for awhile, there was plenty of money from the court settlement. So she had Maggie live with her. Her mother wasn't a burden at all, and she felt guilty to admit her mother was perfect company while she adjusted to life in Tennessee.

Aileen finished the last of the dinner dishes. She wanted nothing more than to retire to the couch and watch something mindless on American TV. There was plenty of mindless programming to watch. It was the perfect way to unwind after spending another day as a dedicated daughter to her aging mother. Maggie stayed in the kitchen, sipping on a cup of tea and listening to an AM talk radio station; she enjoyed listening to the radio over the watching television.

She had just settled into her comfortable sofa and aimed the remote at the TV when Maggie cried out in terror followed by the shattering of broken glass from the kitchen. She sprung from the couch and ran to the kitchen. She feared the worst. Had her mother slipped and fallen? Worse yet, was she having a stroke or heart attack? She arrived to find Maggie cowering against the kitchen cabinets, her hands clutched to her ears. The radio was still on playing a steady low crackle of white noise between stations.

"What's the matter mum?" she asked, trying to hug her.

"I heard the wailing," she said between quick gasps for breath, "the Banshee's cry. Death is upon us Aileen!"

"Banshee?" Aileen asked. "What are you going on about now, mum?"

"The Banshee's cry. I heard it out there." She motioned to the window. "She's out there calling for me."

"Now mum," Aileen said stepping closer to her mother, "you know those are just stories. There are no Banshees. It's going to be okay. It was probably just the wind. Our house sits pretty close to the Bennett's next door. The wind blowing through most likely causes a howling sound every now and again."

Maggie looked into her daughter's eye with serious intensity. "The Banshee is no tall tale. The Banshee is real. She came to take my mum and dad. She took my grandparents and she took your father, my beloved Gerald. Don't be tellin' me there ain't no Banshee. I heard her before and I hear her now."

They were just outside the bathroom door. Maggie stopped and whispered as if there was someone else close she didn't want to hear, "When you hear her cry, one will die. I heard her, Aileen. It's my time, tonight. The Banshee has come for me."

Aileen searched for a better explanation. She was desperate for a better explanation. Her mother was in good health all things considered. She was old but she could manage with her daughter's help. This couldn't be happening, not now. Not tonight. It was all so sudden. She didn't want to be alone.

Aileen never heard the Banshee's wail, but she believed in it. She didn't want to, but deep down she did. Folks had always spoke of the Banshee back in Ireland. She heard the tales as a little girl. They were all the same. Someone heard the cry of the Banshee and the next morning... someone close was gone.

Aileen was shaken by her mother's talk of a Banshee. She wasn't exactly sure what a Banshee was but she was conjuring terrible, monstrous images in her mind. Aileen wanted to to be with her mother during her last moments on Earth. She knew such ideas were ridiculous but she'd also come to know that people from the old country knew things she wasn't prepared to know.

Aileen slept in her mother's bed that night, curled up next to her like she did on moonless nights in Ireland, seeking her mother's warmth and comfort. Eventually fatigue got the best of her and she fell asleep.

When woke in the morning, her hand still clasped firmly in her mother's hands. They were cold as ice. She was gone.

Aileen never could have known her mother's soul had got up in the middle of the night to answer a knock at the door only she could hear.

***

"Are you fucking kidding me with this line?" Vincent Death asked.

Like every room in this crazy building, it was a vast expanse of space tucked within a building that was impossible to contain that much space on a physical level. Vincent Death was learning that a lot of the physics of the world he knew no longer applied to the world in which he now existed.

"Its the morning rush," the Death from Tijuana told him, "but it moves pretty quick. We could have waited for it to thin out but we've got nothing better to do so me might as well just get this over with."

The line moved a step ahead.

"So, do you think they'll assign us together?" Vincent Death asked.

"No. Death always works alone. People think there is only one of us so we have to keep up appearances," the Death from Tijuana told him.

"But, we've been together all day."

"Look, I'm not telling you that we don't team up from time to time. But if we do it's unsanctioned. Sometimes you gotta do what you gotta do out there. The unholy back there behind the desks, making the rules, formulating policies, disciplining the naysayers, they haven't worked a day out there on the the streets. They have no idea what its like. But when you are out there in the shit, you learn to bend the rules when you have to. As long as you get the job done they won't say too much."

"Why'd you call them unholy?"

"Because they haven't done any real work in the field. They haven't got their hands dirty. They haven't put any holes in their Black Tattered Robes™, at least not any more than they were issued with. Unholy."

"I see. So, after I get my assignment we can hook up on the sly? You can help me out with the first few assignments?"

"There is a very real possibility that you are not going to be assigned to Tijuana. In all honesty, you probably won't even receive an assignment within Oaxaca Division. They like to send you to wherever it is you come from typically. Its easier for everyone if you know the terrain, the people. That kind of thing. So, since you're here on vacation, you will probably wind up back around where you came from."

"Great," Vincent Death said, the wind taken out of his sails.

"What?"

"I'll probably wind up back with my wife again."

The line moved up a step.

"You don't need to worry about your wife anymore. Til death do you part. Guess what, your Death. Poof, no marriage. You are no longer contractually obligated."

"You don't know my wife. She never let me out of her sight. Not because she didn't trust me, because she was a control freak who couldn't loosen the reigns for one moment. I'll bet she's pissed right now and is combing all of Tijuana looking for me." A light went on in Vincent Death's head and he reacted as if it were lit with unchecked nuclear power, "Hey, does she become a Death too? Were you supposed to get her as well or did another Death arrive in a timely fashion?"

The Death from Tijuana pursed his rubbery lip bones. "No, I was charged with her as well. Only thing is, the women don't become Death. They become something worse: Banshees" He shivered when he said the word.

"Wanda is a Banshee now? That's what we saw explode out of her grave? That was her?" Vincent asked, piecing it all together and not liking the results very much.

"Yeah, that was her I'm afraid. But, the good news is that is the last time you will ever see her. The Banshees are very solitary. They keep to themselves. They aren't organized like we are. On top of that, Banshees and Deaths don't mix very well. We all do the same type of work and it gets very territorial. Over the years we've both learned to stick to our areas and everyone is happy."

"The Banshees are out there collecting souls as well?"

"Yes. That's why its very important to stick to your assignments and do the job. The Banshees aren't tasked to any souls, they just sort of sniff them out. If you leave any lying around and a Banshee is near she will scoop the job up from you and then there will be a problem. A big problem."

The line moved up a few more steps.

"I thought you said if a soul was left lying around they become me? Or her?"

"They do. The thing is, the Banshees can sniff out a dying soul like a hound dog. They got a sense about it. We rely on the Unholy back there to tell us when the souls get ripe. Worse yet, the cry of a Banshee can induce the death of a soul before its time. Very ugly stuff, the Banshee's wail."

Vincent Death was so engrossed in trying to figure out the new job, he didn't notice that the line had come down to him now.

"Next!" a craggy old Death called from behind a lineup of teller windows much like a bank.

Vincent Death walked up to the craggy old Death clerk ready to receive his assignment. The craggy old Death behind the counter reached across and tapped a scythe blade to Vincent Death's bony hand. The blade glowed and then a printer on the counter began to spit out a ticket. The craggy old Death tore it off at the perforation, examined it for a moment and then slid it across the wooden counter to Vincent Death.

"You've been assigned to the Southeastern U.S. office, Memphis Division. You will report there immediately to receive your charges for the day."

He looked over Vincent Death's shoulder, now finished with his business with him.

"Next!" he yelled, eyeing up Vincent Death still standing at his window like a forgettable piece of vermin that didn't know when to scram before it got swatted.

Vincent Death moved away as the Death from Tijuana reported to the window for his assignment. The craggy old Death repeated the ritual with the scythe blade and the print out. The Death from Tijuana took the paper and walked away from the window without even examining it.

"Hey, what did you get?" Vincent Death asked.

The Death from Tijuana was looking down at the ground. He hadn't even noticed Vincent Death had waited for him. Vincent Death thought he looked shocked that he was even still here.

"Oh, you're still here?" He looked at his assignment for the first time, "Well, looks like I'll be back downtown picking up more tourists. *Always* tourists. That always makes it so hard to lay off the drinks." As an afterthought he added, "So, what'd they give you anyway?"

"Memphis." Vincent Death said, "I'm headed back home."

The Death from Tijuana seemed unimpressed.

"Well, good luck to you then. And uhh, sorry about everything. Really."

Vincent Death was shocked by the sudden end to their friendship. If he could call it that, this was the only Death he really knew and already he was leaving. It all felt sterile and clinical. He offered his hand to shake. The Death from Tijuana looked at him as if he were alien. He didn't understand the gesture at all. Vincent Death stuck his hand back in his robe.

"Hey," Vincent Death said to the Death from Tijuana just before turning to leave, "maybe you better wipe all that paint off your face before you go back out. You look like an idiot."

Vincent Death turned and walked off not waiting for a reply to his smart-assed farewell. It didn't feel like the right thing to do but it felt like the only thing he could do.

Chapter 4: Death Gets a Job

Well, that's great, Vincent Death thought to himself, I have no idea how to get to Memphis.

"Use the book, you dope," a Death said leaning in over his shoulder.

Vincent Death was startled. He looked over his shoulder at the plain-skulled Death. He was indistinguishable from most other Deaths.

How did he read his mind? Is that a power he had also but had not tapped into yet? He was excited that he might be telepathic and didn't know it yet. It was a superpower he always wanted when he was a little boy.

"No, I'm not reading your mind. It's me, from Tijuana! You've forgotten me already?"

"Oh, I didn't recognize you without the sugar skull paint job. How'd you get that off so fast? How'd you know I was thinking I had no idea how to get to Memphis?"

"Wow, you are just full of questions today aren't you? And you standing there like a statue staring off into outer space makes it pretty obvious you have no idea what you're doing." He patted Vincent Death on the chest. "You have the book. Use it. I'm out, peace!"

The plain faced Death from Tijuana stepped back and tapped the wooden handle of his scythe on the ground once. He then shimmered out of sight.

Vincent Death reached into his robe and produced the book out of its special pocket. He thumbed to the back of the book, looking for a glossary. There was one, it took up at least a quarter of the thickness of the entire book. He flipped through the pages to the t's and indexed his finger up and down the columns of words until he found travel. Voila!

The section on travel was pretty extensive. He found a quiet corner in the Assignments office and squatted down with his back to the wall and began to read up on travel. There were so many ways a Death could travel. There were at least twenty pages on simply walking places like everyone else but included important pointers on avoiding being noticed by the living. As it turns out, they can see you even if it's not their time under special circumstances. Mostly they never noticed you unless you did things to get noticed.

Then he got to the section on long distance travel. There is a highway of sorts that Deaths can travel along. It's like another dimension just above and parallel to the dimension the living roam within. Death's scythe acts as a sort of antenna to tap into that system and allow rapid travel to wherever they need to go.

When Vincent Death was satisfied he had the general idea, he stood up. First he stowed the book back in its pocket within the robe. Then he focused his mind on a place he knew in Memphis, the place he knew best, as the book suggested. The stronger your connection to the place the more easily it is to hone in on it. He closed his eyes, which wasn't part of the instructions, and tapped the handle of his scythe with authority to the ground.

His hollow belly went queasy, like he was falling. He felt like he was in an elevator but there was nothing under his feet. He opened his eyes and found himself swirling through a sea of gaseous purple plasma. And then gravity hit him just as fast and the plasma evaporated and he was standing in what appeared to be an employee lounge at some factory. Except, all the employees milling around at lockers and folding tables were all Deaths.

A few regarded him for a fleeting moment. Most didn't seem to notice or care that he had just appeared out of thin air. He felt ignored at first but realized they must see Deaths come and go like that all the time. It was unremarkable to them. Vincent Death wondered how long before all this would become unremarkable to him.

"Hey, new guy!" a Death called out with a gusto Vincent Death had yet to hear uttered from the maw of a reaper. "Five minutes to shift start. Better grab your assignment pronto, partner!"

He looked over to the source of the voice and saw a cowboy in black. The reaper was wearing the signature Black Tattered Robe™ but instead of his hood pulled over his head, he wore a great black cowboy hat that did an equally good job of obscuring his skeletal facial features as the hood. He also sported a thick, moppy gray mustache that hid his mouth and wriggled like a caterpillar when he spoke. Also, it was impossible not to notice the pointy black leather cowboy boots darting out from under the robe complete with gun metal black spurs that chimed at the slightest movement.

"I don't know where the assignments office is. Could you point out the direction?" Vincent Death asked Cowboy Death.

"Sure partner! I'd be happy to!"

The cowboy Death put his arm around Vincent Death's neck like they were lifelong pals, and walked him out of the break room. He thought the cowboy Death's arms felt bigger and burlier than they should be for a skeleton.

"Are we going to be partners?" Vincent Death asked.

The cowboy Death laughed big and genuine like Vincent Death had told him a great joke. "No hombre, I call everyone partner, partner. It's just an expression. Like my dogs are barkin' or my biscuits are burnin' or my wolves are howlin'. Stuff like that, partner. Get it?"

"Yeah, I get it."

The halls of the Memphis office were just like those in Oaxaca: long, narrow and straight. So plain they gave a sense of disorientation. The walls were peppered with doors that Vincent Death was sure opened into rooms that did not fit the geometry of the building. The cowboy Death steered him to an unmarked, plain wooden door.

"Here we are partner, Assignment Office. Well, I gotta mount up and ride! There's souls to drive out there! Be seein' ya partner."

"Yeah, be seeing you," Vincent Death said with a wave. He kind of liked the boisterous cowboy Death. He was hoping he would see him again soon.

Vincent Death opened the door to the Assignment Office. Before he could step in the doorway, he was getting yelled at for being late.

"Let's go! Let's go! You only have a minute and a half until shift start! What are you waiting for, Death? Are you going to be a problem for me already?"

Vincent Death walked into the office, his tail tucked between his legs. He apologized for being tardy (even though he wasn't technically) and tried to explain that he had just come all the way from Tijuana where he received only rudimentary training. He knew it just sounded like he was making excuses for himself even as he spoke, but they were all valid excuses.

"Yeah, yeah yeah," the clerk said disinterested, "did you get the book?"

"Yes," Vincent Death said.

"Good." The clerk shoved a piece of paper at him. "Here is your assignment for the day. Sixteen seconds to shift. You got a job, get a move on."

Vincent Death looked at the paper. There was only one item on it. Margaret O'Kelly. Below the name was a location. It was an address that seemed familiar to him. He struggled to understand why the address was ringing a bell. It hit him, the street name was the street he lived on when he was a living being. It had felt like only hours ago that Vincent Death was alive, or at least a part of the land of the living and not whatever it was he was a part of now.

Vincent Death used his limited training and focused on his old neighborhood. He closed his eyes and tapped his scythe to the floor. He was transported through the queasy purple plasma, and when the disorienting feeling stopped and his feet were on solid, tangible ground again he opened his eyes.

It felt like a giant cement fist had punched him in the gut. The wind that he no longer breathed was knocked out of his chest. He was looking at the front of the house he once lived in. He knew right away that was a thing of the past even if it was the recent past. He last saw it just two days ago when he and his wife had left for Tijuana. Now he was back and looking at it through hollow black eye cavities.

This wasn't where he was supposed to be. The house address he was supposed to retrieve the soul from was where his former next door neighbors live. A nice Irish family that were new to the neighborhood if he remembered correctly. He never did get a chance to meet them so it was nice that this was his first assignment.

A new found brazenness overcame him. He was Death now. The living couldn't tell him what to do anymore. And if he did something people didn't like, well, what were they going to do about it anyway? So he sauntered right across his former neighbor's front lawn. Fuck them. He rang the doorbell.

***

Maggie heard the doorbell ring. What time was it? It felt too late or too early for someone to be at the front door. After last night's affair with the Banshee wail, she was too spooked to answer the door for herself.

She knew the Banshees were just superstition from the old country. She knew she shouldn't be believing in such things and she probably didn't believe it in her heart of hearts until she heard that baleful crying last night. She heard an actual Banshee cry before; to her it was unmistakable what the source of such an awful noise could be.

Now, however, in the early morning twilight the silly thoughts we think in the dark were beginning to evaporate. But not enough for her to want to get up and see who was at the door. Was someone really at the door? Perhaps she was just hearing things. She stayed still.

The bell rang a third time.

"Oh, I'm just being silly," Maggie said aloud

to herself. The sound of her own voice kept her company and helped clear the heebie-jeebies she was having.

Maggie fought back the pain in her arthritic legs and made her way down the hall from her room to see who was at the front door. The bell rang a fourth time and now she was becoming more annoyed than scared

"I'm coming," she called out again so she could hear her own voice and chase away the remaining fears,."I'm an old lady, you're just going to have to wait a moment!"

When she got to the door, she looked into the living room just across the way. She saw the TV was on and the rest of the family was sitting on the couch motionless. Maggie's hand was on the door knob. As she twisted it open she thought it was odd how the rest of the family was sitting there, like in a snapshot. It was like they were frozen in time and the only thing fluid was her.

She swung the door open as she thought those queer thoughts. She turned to see who the pest was ringing the doorbell so early in the morning.

Death was at her doorstep.

***

"It's time to go, Maggie," Vincent Death

said. He wanted his first official words as Death to be poignant yet quotable. But that was all that he blurted out when the old woman opened the door.

She didn't say anything. She looked surprised but resigned to her fate, like she knew he would be there. But she just stood there, looking at him.

Panic walloped him when he realized he had no idea what happened next. Was he supposed to just yank her out of the house? Was there some sort of protocol for getting the charges to follow you? And just where was he supposed to take her to? Back to the office? That somehow didn't seem right.

"Ahhh, hang on a second," he said holding up a finger.

The woman continued to just look at him in silence but now it was the look people give to children when they are doing something so insane as to lack any logical progression. She placed her hands on her hips like she was angry that he was wasting her time. She should be grateful, Vincent Death thought to himself, I'm actually buying her some time here.

He pulled out the book. He thumbed through the pages trying to zero in the section about where he should be taking Maggie. Her impatience and his lack of professionalism were causing him to fumble a lot more than he should be. It felt like it was taking decades to hone in on the information.

Then came the wail like a steam locomotive. Low at first but getting louder and closer at a rapid rate. Before either of them could react to the awful crying bearing down on them, Vincent Death was tackled to the ground by a black-blue blur that came in from his left. He and the blur rolled off Maggie's front porch and into the bushes.

As quick as he had been taken down, the thing was up and off him. Vincent Death propped himself up on one elbow trying to see what had just happened. He looked back up at the porch and the thing grabbed Maggie by the wrist, yanking her out the door. The thing turned its head and looked at Vincent as it clutched Maggie to its body like prey. A look came over the thing's face, like it recognized something about Vincent Death that it didn't notice before. Then it hissed at Vincent Death and its mouth contorted into a ghastly open maw, and the awful cry shrieked out as it zapped off and away from the porch.

Vincent Death recognized the motion right away. It was the same way that thing shot out of his wife's grave in Tijuana and vanished into the sky. And that was because the other thing he recognized was that that thing was his wife. And his wife recognized him too, of that he was sure.

There was another problem, Vincent Death realized as he got himself up off the ground and out of the bushes. His wife just took off with his charge. It was his very first job and she fucked it all up. Even in death, she was ruining his life.

Chapter 5: Death Gets a Divorce

The Banshee knew her foe. She knew him well. It was her good-for-nothing husband Vincent. He thought he could hide from her. He thought he could get away from her. Bullshit to that, she thought.

Wanda had forgotten all about him while dealing with what felt like the worst bout of PMS she had ever experienced. It was bad enough she thought that grim reaper was trying to steal the soul she was attached to, but when she saw her husband masquerading around as Death, that set her over the edge. She wanted to rip out his guts. How dare he try to get away from her by pretending to be dead. In the end, the only thing that stopped her was the compulsion to take this soul that was attached to her. Take her away from here and bring it to The River.

She had no idea what compelled her to do so, but the tug was strong just like the raw emotion that was driving her. It was almost maternal like. A need to protect this soul that attached itself to her when it heard her crying. She pulled the soul to her bosom and flew to The River. She had never been there but she knew the way. Something internal guided her like a salmon on its final run up a river it had not known since it was a hatchling.

She would return to deal with her husband in

due time. He would not get away from her that easy. She cried again as she shrieked across the sky. The soul of Maggie clutched to her bosom caressed her, trying to comfort her. She looked upon the peaceful face of Maggie's soul; it was weeping and trying to comfort her. This only made Wanda cry harder, she would never find comfort.

There was a fold in the sky just ahead of her. She flew into it. All of a sudden everything became dark and calm. The sound of air that whooshed past them had ceased. No air currents pushed back at them as they shot across the sky. The land passing by below them was rocky and mostly barren. The few trees that still stood looked dead and charred. Ahead of them a great river could be seen cutting across the landscape with only pure blackness beyond its banks.

She saw twin fires burning through the darkness at the edge of the great river. The orange flames danced on the banks, their mirror images dancing along in the reflection off the inky black waters of the river. The Banshee honed in on that spot.

She glided in on the fires like an airplane lining up on the lights of a runway. Up close, she could see the fires were fueled by two stacks of deadfall. Logs and twigs alike burned in each pile. There was a skiff floating still on the river, framed perfectly by the two fires. A figure stood in shadow at the aft of the flat decked boat. It was cloaked and held a punting pole. It stood as motionless as the waters it floated upon.

The Banshee brought the soul of Maggie to the twin fires and set her down. Without hesitation, Maggie stepped onto the bow of the skiff. The Banshee waited to see Maggie off. This was her first soul, she figured she owed the moment at least the chance to see her off.

The boatman didn't move a muscle.

Perhaps he's waiting for the skiff to fill, the Banshee thought to herself. She scanned the barren lands around the boat landing. Not another soul in sight. She was second guessing the need for savoring this moment.

The boatman on the skiff turned his head to look at the Banshee. He extended an arm out from his robe. He crackled like aged wicker as he moved. In his hand he held a coin purse and he jingled it at the Banshee.

"What? I gotta pay you now?" she cried at the boatman. "Are you freaking kidding me? You should be paying me. I'm the one who brought her here, I did all the work. All you gotta do is row, row, row your little boat across the river and you're done. How dare you!"

The boatman only jingled his coin purse at her in response.

The Banshee sighed. "Okay, how much you fucking con artist? I'll pay you this once but let's get something straight so we are both clear for next time. I'll be the one charging for labor around here, not you. Next time you are going to pay me!"

Again, the boatman jingled his purse.

The Banshee felt around her clothing. She had no money. She looked around the pebbly ground, perhaps someone dropped a quarter on the ground the last time this crook hassled someone for change. Nothing.

The boatman jingled his purse at her, this time seeming to indicate something on her. She took the idea of where he was wagging his sack at her and realized he was interested in the gold ring that adorned her mummified finger. Her wedding ring.

"Oh no! You're not getting this! This is mine. It was given to me and I suffered a lifetime for it."

The boatman crackled like broken twigs as he tucked his coin purse back inside his robe. He pointed at Maggie at the bow of the boat, who was oblivious to the argument taking place. She looked to the other side of the river like a child eager to take a road trip. Then the boatman pointed back to the Banshee. He wanted her off his skiff.

The Banshee threw her hands in the air and retrieved Maggie off the skiff.

The twin fires died out. The boatman used his punting pole to pilot the skiff away from the landing. He floated away downriver. The Banshee and Maggie were left standing in the dark on the shore of the River Styx.

Now what the hell was she going to do?

***

Vincent Death had no idea what the hell he was going to do. It was his first day on the job and already he'd lost his first charge to his ex-wife, a Banshee. He wasn't sure what the policy on that one was but he was pretty sure they were going to frown upon that sort of thing.

Maggie was the only soul he was given to retrieve. He wasn't ready to tuck his tail between his legs and report back to the office. He had to think, he wanted to be good at this Death business. There had to be a way.

Before he had time to begin percolating a plan, Maggie's front door opened. The woman on the other side went pie-eyed when she saw the skeleton donned in a Tattered Black Robe™ at her doorstep.

Vincent Death felt moths flutter around inside his shriveled dead heart. He was struck by the woman's emerald green eyes. They sparkled like jewels in a dimly lit cave and their brilliance shook Vincent Death right to the core. Only her angelic voice broke his trance.

"You're—" she said, the sound of her voice stolen away by the shock of recognition.

"Death," Vincent Death confirmed.

She let loose a scream that could shatter

double paned glass. In response, Vincent yowled his own version; the two could have shattered a wine glass had one been nearby.

"My... my mother! My mother! Oh God. No! You can't have her!" the lady spat.

"I don't want her." Vincent Death paused. "No, well I do but, well, someone else has her."

Vincent Death was flabbergasted. He'd come to do a job, but now, looking into this panicked woman's beautiful eyes, all he wanted to do was figure out a way to get to know her better.

An idea struck him right in the head. Not an idea in the abstract form but an idea in the form of a big, thick, meaty book. Vincent Death toppled over, he was not expecting to get hit in the head with something the size of a phone book.

"What the hell?" he said, dazed from the sneak attack. He looked around, rubbing his head, to see who threw the book at him.

Cowboy Death took two steps closer to Vincent Death, his spurs ringing like jingle bells with each step. He made a big throaty sound and hocked a ball of phlegm into the bushes next to where Vincent Death was sitting. Then the Cowboy Death hooked his thumbs into the thick leather belt fastened around the waist of his Tattered Black Robe™.

"I knew you was gonna have troubles the moment I laid eyes on ya, partner," Cowboy Death said.

"A Banshee just stole my charge. She's my wife," Vincent Death said. "Ex-wife," he corrected himself, sounding more hopeful than convinced.

"No shit. That's why I threw the book at ya. It's all in there. It's ain't pretty neither. They don't take kindly to you losing charges. Worse, it was a Banshee that took your charge. Likely means a long trip to Limbo for ya, partner."

"Limbo? I thought that's where lost souls went?"

"Technically, yes. But, that's the western block. The eastern block of Limbo is where all the bad Deaths go to be punished. Look, on the bright side though, at least they won't erase your soul."

"The bright side? Erase my soul? What's that supposed to mean?" Vincent Death said, his voice cracking from fright.

"Erasing your soul, that's death for Deaths. There's no coming back from that one."

"There's two of you?" the woman at the door yelled. "And what's this about a Banshee?"

Vincent Death was envisioning an unpleasant life for his new existence as Death. He wanted to cry like a scared little boy. This was not fair at all. He'd hardly received any training and he felt thrown to the dogs. Now he felt the dogs had mauled him to shreds. He put his head between his knees and covered the back of his head with his skeleton hands trying to hide himself from his new world.

"Hello?" the beautiful lady at the front door called out, perturbed she was being ignored by the two grim reapers at her doorstep.

Vincent Death popped up. He had a plan and he didn't need the book.

He grabbed the woman by the hand. "I swear to you... I didn't get your name?"

"Aileen."

"I swear to you, Aileen, I will get your mother back from the Banshee. I can't bring her back to you, her time is up. But I will bring her to the hereafter as she was meant."

Aileen nodded, a tear rolling down her cheek. "The Banshee, we heard it last night. I didn't believe my mother but now I know it's true. Oh, she was so frightened when she heard that awful wailing. Please, rescue her from that terrible monster. I need to know she went in peace."

"I swear this to you, Aileen. I will be back."

Still clinging to Aileen's hand, he looked over his shoulder at Cowboy Death. He was a lifeline (or Deathline to be more accurate).

He let go of Aileen's hand. It was time to get down to business. He picked up The Book and opened it. He scanned the pages not knowing exactly what he was looking for other than a way out of this mess.

Cowboy Death came up alongside of him. He reached in and flipped the book open to the section he wanted Vincent Death to read. He scanned back a few pages, paused, then turned a few pages ahead and pointed at a passage for Vincent Death to read.

Vincent Death had seen that the margins of this book were marked up with lots of handwritten notes and even some odd sketches. He could have sworn he even saw a lewd doodle or two as Cowboy Death turned the pages. The book struck Vincent Death as something belonging to a high school kid. He read aloud when Cowboy Death pointed to a paragraph on the page.

"The job is completed when a soul, in name, has been guided to the Hereafter. Once verification of receipt is received from Hereafter officials, Death will be credited with a retrieval on his permanent record. All jobs must be completed by day's end."

"See," Cowboy Death said, "all we gotta do is find you a Maggie O'Kelly."

Vincent Death was confused. "But, the Banshee just took Maggie O'Kelly. That's the problem."

"No, no, no. Not the Maggie O'Kelly. A Maggie O'Kelly. Didn't you pay attention to what you read? A soul...in name. It's a loophole. All they check for is that you delivered a soul named Maggie O'Kelly to the Hereafter by the end of the day."

"I have to kill someone named Maggie

O'Kelly whose time isn't necessarily up?" Vincent Death asked, catching up to the cowboy's plan.

"Better her than you is what I'm saying," Cowboy Death whispered with a tip of his hat. He gave Aileen a reassuring wink.

"*I can't do that to her*!" Vincent Death whispered under his own breath. "I just made her a promise. I need *her* mother, not *a* mother! I won't do it like this!"

"Oh alright, the banshee is your ex-wife you say?" Cowboy Death asked.

Vincent Death nodded in the affirmative.

"Then she's as wet behind the ears as you are. There is a chance she's made a common mistake most Banshees make."

Cowboy Death turned to Aileen and asked, "Did your mother have a wedding ring or some other type of valuable that was the most precious thing to her?"

"Yes. Her wedding ring is still in her room. She hasn't worn it since my father passed away. She keeps it in a locked box."

"We're going to need that ring."

"That'll bring her back here?" Aileen asked.

"No," Cowboy Death said. "It will give us leverage."

***

"I'll be back, Aileen. I promise," Vincent

Death said.

He held her warm hand in his boney hand. His empty eye sockets lingered on her lush green eyes for a moment longer. The he let go of her hand and tapped his scythe on the ground.

He was whisked away along the purple haze highway that only Deaths can travel along. He was queasy again, feeling like he was riding an elevator that plummeted in all directions at once somehow.

He landed firmly on his feet in a dark and charred world. This wasn't Earth, it was Elsewhere.

"Come on!" Cowboy Death said.

He had arrived ahead of Vincent Death, not caring to wait around for the mushy goodbye with Aileen.

Ahead of them twin pyres smoldered in the shadows. Two shadowy figures stood between them. It was Maggie and the Banshee. Cowboy and Vincent Death raced to them, never setting foot on the ground, they hovered and made the span between them in the flash of a lightning bolt.

"Maggie," Vincent Death said, holding out his hand to the kidnapped soul, "come with us. We can deliver you to eternity."

The Banshee hissed at the two Deaths. She grabbed Maggie by the arm and clutched her close. Her ragged robes inflated around her and enveloped Maggie like the hug of a gelatinous octopus.

"Vincent you bastard!" The Banshee wailed, "You come here this instant! This is all your fault! I need money to get that lazy boatman to take this woman away!"

"She is not yours to take, Banshee. And neither am I. 'Til death did we part and I am Death now, I have no further obligation to you. Enough is enough, what you are doing is bigger than us. It's bigger than our rocky marriage that we held in our mortal form. You are rocking the boat between our kinds, the Deaths and the Banshees."

The Banshee puffed up. "Did you just call me Banshee? How dare you, Vincent! I am your wife! Call me Wanda! My name is Wanda!"

The Banshee levitated a few more feet higher. Maggie's feet dangled off the ground as the Banshee kept her locked close to her body like a child clutching a teddy bear. A small storm began to brew around her. She was furious but had no idea how to let her anger out at Vincent Death.

Vincent Death was just about to run away from the creature that was once his wife. Fear of her causing him physical harm still lingered somewhere deep inside him. Cowboy Death reacted to the Banshee's temper tantrum before Vincent Death lost his cool.

The Cowboy Death produced Maggie's wedding ring from inside his Black Tattered Robe™. The Banshee plopped back down to the ground like a toy helicopter with a dead battery.

"Give it to me! That's the ring the boatman wanted!" the Banshee wailed.

"Oh no," Cowboy Death said, "this is not a bargaining chip. This is proof the soul belongs to us."

"Give me the ring now!"

The Banshee reached out and grabbed Cowboy Death's wrist. She let go of Maggie with her other hand and reached out to grab the ring from Cowboy Death's skeletal hand. Cowboy Death countered by locking his free hand around the Banshee's wrist. The stared into each other's cold, dead eyes with disdain. They were dead locked in each other's grip.

"Grab Maggie! Now!" Cowboy Death said to Vincent Death.

Cowboy Death leaned into the Banshee and wrestled her down to the ground. The Banshee was caught off guard by the Death's move and found herself pinned to the ground. She was more concerned with getting Maggie back in her grip now that she realized she let go of her in a moment of rage. She fought to get out from under Death's grip and get to Maggie before her husband could.

But all three stopped when they heard what sounded like a flock of screaming pterodactyls come racing in from behind them. They all looked in the direction of the screams to see a dark streaking cloud racing right toward them. It moved so quickly it was on them before they could take cover.

Vincent Death thought it was a flock of humongous crows. He shielded his head and swatted at the air just before he reached Maggie. He realized it wasn't a murder of crows swooping in on them. It was a squadron on Banshees.

They buzzed down low, forcing Vincent to the ground. As their collective siren screech receded, he saw they had scooped up Maggie and his ex-wife, the Banshee, as well. He looked to the ground across from him and saw Cowboy Death with his belly to the ground too.

Vincent Death felt his ashen heart skip a beat. They had Maggie at their fingertips and lost her.

Cowboy Death grinned at him, his skeleton face grinning from behind the cowboy hat that never fell off his head during all the commotion.

He offered his hand out to Vincent Death and unfurled his fist. He still had the ring.

Chapter 6: A Death in the Shitter

Wanda writhed in the clutch of the Banshee who had snagged her. She was trying to break free of their grasp. She had a new strength she'd not had before, and was able to wiggle free of the Banshee holding her. There were easily a dozen of them flying in a tight formation; it was as if Wanda were suspended in a black cloud. She broke free of one only to be held by another.

They were flying rapidly through the air but Wanda could not feel so much as a breeze on her face. She could not tell where they were going but the burnt red ember tone of the landscape soon transformed into an ember ethereal glow around here. Wanda ceased her struggles and allowed herself to be taken to wherever it was they were taking her.

The black cloud of Banshees touched down in a circle of brilliant green light. The Banshees released their grip and stepped away from her, forming a circular wall of their own just inside the wall of green light. As they backed away, she saw the soul of Maggie. The Banshees had taken her too.

"What are you doing with us? Let us go this instant, I must get this woman to the boat!" Wanda demanded.

"She will get to the boats. That's why we've brought you here," one of the Banshees wailed.

The crying speech of the Banshee grated her eardrums like fingers on a chalk board. The sound of the Banshee's cry was worse than the screeches of a child that doesn't get their way. Wanda didn't want to hear another syllable of it.

"Our voices are awful. We shirk from the sound of it. In time you will learn to tolerate it like a painful limp. It is important for you to learn to deal with it if the plan is to work," the Banshee said. Wanda wasn't able to tell which one spoke; all their faces were pulled back into a mournful scowl, an expression that never seemed to leave any of their faces.

"Plan? What plan?" Wanda asked, becoming cognizant of the terrible sound of her own voice.

"Our kind has always been solitary. It is the nature of our being," the Banshee explained. "But that has hindered our progression. In the meantime, the Deaths have learned to organize. They worked together for eons and they are a threat to our very existence.

"We struggle for scraps. We scavenge for lost souls, forgotten souls, worthless souls. The pickings are slim and hardly sustain us. Simply put, we are becoming extinct.

"There is a revolution forming. This squadron you see before you has learned to coexist. We've learned to overcome our need to be solitary and we've taught ourselves to tolerate the baleful sounds of each other voices, the way a vampire learns to resist the urge for warm human blood. It is not easy but the sacrifices we make are essential for our existence.

"You have unwittingly launched the first shot of the war. You have taken this soul from the League. You did not know it but you've drawn a line in the sand and the Deaths now know they can not simply lay claim to souls and take them. Now there is competition, it will no longer be easy for them.

"They will not give up that easily. This will be a war from here on out. We must find more of our kind and recruit them and grow our numbers before the Deaths destroy the groundwork we've laid. Every step we take right now will determine the outcome of this war. Victory is in our grasp if we keep our minds to it.

"We will get your soul, Maggie, on the ferryman's boat. You have no idea about any of this. I know it is hard for you to process right now but you are the most important Banshee ever to soar through the ether. We will teach you all you need to know and you will grow to become the most powerful Banshee ever to cry out in anger and sorrow."

Wanda was trying to process it all. She felt like she was being born again. It started when she realized she sounded as awful as these other Banshees. The Banshee's speech put it over the top and now she stood there realizing what she refused to acknowledge all along: she was dead. She was a banshee. That is why she was acting the way she was, incapable of handling her raging emotions

Now, unlike in life, she stood before people who believed they could harness her rage. They understood the potential of her anger. They respected her ability to strike fear into the hearts of those who would dare challenge her.

"What do we need to do?" Wanda the Banshee asked.

Though she knew this squadron of Banshees had trained themselves to deal with the terrible sounds of their own voices, she saw they all were having some trouble adjusting to her voice. She believed she was more powerful than all of them combined. She knew in that moment this flock would be her new spouse and she would be their matron.

"First, we need to get that ring," the lead Banshee said.

***

"I'm in deep shit. I'll never get Maggie back now," Vincent Death said.

"Well, there is some good news," Cowboy Death said.

"What good news could there be?"

"It's only ten a.m. We still have most of the day to get her back."

Vincent Death stomped his foot and got right up in the brim of Cowboy Death's hat.

"How are we supposed to get Maggie away from a whole brood of those things?"

"Is there a mouse in your pocket?" Cowboy Death asked, calm and unnerved by the agitated Death screaming in his face.

"Huh?" Vincent Death asked.

"What's this we shit? Maggie is your problem. Don't you forget that. I'm along for the ride to help you out, but this is your ship. You better stop leaning on me for advice on everything. It's time for you to start coming up with some ideas. Just because I've been at this longer than you doesn't mean I have all the answers. You've got as good a shot at making the right call as I do. There's no chapter in The Book about this scenario, I assure you."

Vincent Death realized he had been expecting Cowboy Death to instruct him every step of the way. He was never going to make it as a Death if he couldn't think on his feet. He had no idea how to solve a problem he never encountered before. He was going to need to spitball some ideas and see if any stuck. Though Vincent Death never had to do this as a grim reaper, he could still recall how he would come up with solutions to his problems in life.

"Got a newspaper?" Vincent Death asked Cowboy Death.

"What in tarnation are you talking about boy?" Cowboy Death asked.

"Never mind. I just need you to get me to a bathroom. I've gotta go real bad."

"Bathroom?" Cowboy Death let a guffaw out. "Deaths don't have bodily function anymore. You don't have to go to the bathroom. You're just scared shitless is what you are!"

"No. I'm not. I'm ready to tackle this but I need to sit on the head awhile and ponder the options."

Cowboy Death shrugged. "Okay, the crapper it is if that's what you insist. Grab on."

Vincent Death put his hand on Cowboy Death's shoulder and they shimmered back onto the purple highway. Vincent Death became disoriented again, but less so this time. He was getting used to this way of traveling.

They materialized back in real time in the grimy corner of a smoky pub. Vincent Death figured they were back on Earth's plane. The bar was crowded with people but it was poorly lit and they were difficult to see standing in the corner in their Tattered Black Robes™. Vincent Death was also realizing that people simply didn't notice Deaths walking among them, unless it was time, of course.

"A bar?" Vincent Death asked.

"It's got a shitter, hombre. Besides, I like hanging out at this place. Reminds me of the old days. Go git doing what you gotta do, I'm gonna mingle." Cowboy Death said and sauntered off, the sound of his heel spurs jingled as he hovered off.

Vincent Death made his way toward the back of the bar where he figured the bathrooms would be located. He was worried that with a crowd this size he wouldn't have enough alone time with his thoughts before some drunken frat boy tried to barge his way in to take a colossal alcohol infused piss.

It was that thought that floated through the empty cavity in his head when a midget, flying through the air, careened into him. The force of the midget cannon-balling into him threw him against the wall. The midget was small, as midgets go, and the only thing that wound up hurting was his pride.

Vincent teetered, attempting to get up but found his Tattered Black Robe™ was sticking to the wall like it was coated in two-day old grape jelly. Vincent Death leveraged his skeleton hand against the wall to free himself and found that it was worse than jelly, it was Velcro.

"Look where you're going, asshole!" one of the drunken bar patrons yelled.

"C'mon you cock-dick, get outta the way, we're trying to play here!" cajoled another.

The midget grabbed Vincent Death by the arm and helped pull him free of the wall.

"Let's go, before they kick your ass," the midget said.

Vincent Death felt his Tattered Black

Robe™ tear free of the wall. He winced, fearing it would tatter beyond regulation tattering but it appeared to remain intact as a tattered black robe could. He turned his attention back to his would-be midget rescuer and realized he too was wearing a Tattered Black Robe™ only his was much smaller.

"You're Death?" Vincent Death asked.

"Bathroom. Now!" Midget Death said, tugging Vincent Death back toward the back hall of the pub.

"You're a Death!" Vincent Death repeated.

Midget Death led Vincent Death into the restroom at the back of the pub. The bathroom was small, just enough room to fit two emaciated Deaths in its confines. There was a sink on the wall that was once white but was now looked like the pallid skin of a person on their deathbed. The toilet was backed up with the remnants of a thousand bottles of stale beer and the product of every Tuesday night all-you-can-eat wings party for the past month.

"You're a Death. A little Death." Vincent Death said like he'd just discovered a talking frog.

"Yes. You've said that several times now," Midget Death said, sliding over the latch on the door and not having much faith that it would hold up if an antsy patron wanted to make a case for who has to use the facilities more urgently.

"Are you going to blow me? Why are we in the bathroom?" Vincent Death asked as if he realized he was in the bathroom all of a sudden.

"No! I'm not going to blow you, though I should. You're famous, or infamous depending on how you look at things."

"Huh? What do you mean?"

"Listen Rookie, you're making waves already. Word on the ether is you've got an entire squadron of Banshees after you. Not just one, a whole squadron!"

"After me? More like I'm after them!" Vincent Death retorted.

"That's not how I hear it. There's a buzz, a war is afoot. The Banshee's have rallied and organized. I've heard you lost your charge to them, they've drawn a line in the sand. This is unprecedented. They are making their stand against Death and you're the poster boy for their cause.

"And I'm going to be honest. If the rumors are true, the worst place you could find yourself right now is hanging out in a bar that caters to frat boys who enjoy throwing midgets at Velcro walls. I want to believe the rumors are just that, rumors. I want to believe you're here because you've just handed your charge over to Charon and you are here celebrating with your cowboy compadre after a long day at the office.

"The last thing I want to believe is that a Death has lost its charge to an army of Banshees and the most important thing that Death can think to do is show up at a seedy bar to take a crap. Please tell me the rumors aren't true."

Vincent Death looked side to side not wanting to meet Midget Death's expectant gaze. He tapped his foot and thought of how best to explain himself. Despite Midget Death's diminutive size, he swayed with an air of authority.

"The rumors aren't true," Vincent Death said, trying his best to sound convincing.

"Thank goodness," Midget Death said and sounded surprised and relieved at the same time.

"Not entirely, anyway," Vincent Death added.

"What?" Midget Death asked, slumping his shoulders.

"Well, I did lose my charge. But only to one Banshee!"

"Okay, well, that's still not good but not unheard of. It can be remedied."

"Well, I did try to remedy that. Me and Cowboy Death kicked that Banshee's ass."

"Oh, great! So this whole sordid mess is over."

"Well, no," Vincent Death said and paused realizing this was the punch he wanted to pull but now he couldn't. "That's when the squadron came and snatched my charge and the other Banshee and flew off."

Midget Death smacked his face and let his hand slide down the side of his skull. He looked like he was imitating Lou Costello and it would have been adorable had the situation not actually warranted that reaction.

"What, in the name of Hades, are you doing hanging around in a bar, may I ask? Because, right now, you are about to fuck everything up for everyone."

"I... I ahhh... came here to think things out on the shitter."

Midget Death metered his words to the non-existent sound of a metronome swinging at an adagio pace. "You came here to think things out on the shitter."

"Yeah."

Midget Death exploded like a thunderhead. "You are Death! You can't shit anymore! What good is thinking on the shitter going to do you? You have the book, you have a problem. Consult the book. Better yet, consider what it is that give the Banshee its power."

Vincent Death chewed on that. When Wanda died, that gave her the power to be a Banshee. Could death itself be the source of her power or just the catalyst for her being. She could fly. Were there some sort of wings she had that he hadn't noticed and all he would have to do would be to cut them off? She went from epic bitch to super epic bitch when she became a Banshee, perhaps her anger is what gave her power. Maybe Banshees were all just a bunch of mega bitches? Vincent Death wished he could just sit on the bowl only for a moment; he was sure the answer would come to him.

There was a loud hammering on the bathroom door. Boom! Boom! Boom!

"Hey, give us back our midget or I'll come in there and beat your ass!" the voice on the other side of the door yelled.

"Well, I better get back to the midget toss before they bust in here and kick your ass. They are rather fond of me as I'm the lightest one they have in their arsenal. They can really get good arc with me. They have a great time and I have a great time watching how happy they are to whip me at the Velcro wall. You need some happy time when you're dealing in the death business all the time, otherwise the job can drag you down after awhile.

"Oh and here," Midget Death reached into his tiny Black Tattered Robe™, retrieved an object and tossed it to Vincent Death, "take this. It's not in the book but I'm sure you'll find it will come in handy."

Vincent Death caught the object and examined it as Midget Death unlatched the door and rejoined the group of drunken frat boys and their silly game of midget tossing. It was a roll of silver duct tape. Of course. Duct tape fixed everything! He didn't need a toilet, he needed a talisman! The duct tape would serve as a constant reminder that Vincent Death could fix anything.

With a renewed sense of purpose and grit determination, Vincent Death exited the shitter. He found Cowboy Death who was standing against the wall and nursing a mug of beer. His beard was curved up into a smile. Vincent Death realized Cowboy Death was eyeing the the posterior end of two young ladies whose rear ends were in the prime of their life. Vincent Death took in an eyeful for himself as well.

"It's good to be dead. I could sit here all day and look at those perfect buns and they would be none the wiser. I may not have Earthly male desires any longer but a good ass is a good ass. No libido needed for that level of enjoyment, no sir," Cowboy Death mused as Vincent Death came shoulder to shoulder with him. "Did the shitter work for you?"

"You could say that," Vincent Death said.

"I did say that. So we can go, partner?"

"We can go."

"Okay. Where to?"

"We need to find a Death who hasn't picked up their charge yet."

"Why?"

"So we can let the Banshees steal the charge."

"That's your plan?" Cowboy Death said, peeling his eyes of the asses.

Vincent Death held up his talisman, "Duct tape, baby!"

Chapter 7: A Death In Salem

Vincent Death thought Cowboy Death had made a wrong turn in Albuquerque. Not only did their surroundings indicate they may not be in the right place, they also looked like they had traveled to the wrong time. Everything looked colonial era and Gothic to boot.

One house in particular stood out like a sore thumb. It was covered in black clapboard with steep pointed gables. Vincent Death felt a chill through his bones just looking at it and figured that was saying a lot since he was Death. The sign hung from a post on the front lawn did not help put Vincent Death at ease.

"Are you sure we're at the right place?" Vincent Death asked.

"Yes siree! This is it! If you're looking for a Death who hasn't got his charge for the day, outside of you of course, this is the place you'll find him for certain," Cowboy Death told him.

"Are we even here, in the now?" Vincent Death asked.

"What in blazes are you going on about boy? This is it, this is the place!"

Vincent Death pointed to the ominous sign. "Witch House? You're telling me there's still witches?"

"Ahh that. Well, don't mind that none, that's just for the edification of the tourists, you see. There's signs like that all over Salem. Now I ain't saying there ain't no such thing as witches because there are. In fact, that's why I knew to come here."

"So we're in Salem, Massachusetts and there are still witches here?"

"Yeah, that's right. Pesky little critters them witches. Poor Death stationed here has his work cut out for him. There's some downright nasty witches here. They just love to repel Death. It's like sport to them. They don't make his job easy at all."

An old man, well into his nineties, raced past Vincent Death and Cowboy Death like he was Usain Bolt. The scene had all the comedic timing of a classic Marx Brothers film, given their conversation. After the old man shot past them, there was a rhythmic *tap, tap, tap* sound of bone on brick behind them as a Death ran past trying to catch the old man. They could hear the old man hoot with delight in the distance.

"See?" Cowboy Death said. "The witches are always fucking with him."

"Okay, so if that Death can't catch him then we can't catch him. What about the Banshees? Does the witches' magic affect them? Will they be unable to catch him also?"

"Oh, the witches' magic doesn't affect us or the Banshees. But it will affect the humans and their souls. This is the kind of shenanigans them witches pull, dangling charges out like carrots," Cowboy Death said.

The old man came skipping past them from the opposite direction now. He cried, "Wheee!" as he went past. Then the *tap, tap, tap* of bone of brick again and the Salem Death darted past them as well. "Afternoon fellas," he said to them as he passed.

"Shouldn't that Death be in Limbo by now for missing all these charges, day in and day out?" Vincent Death asked.

"Nah, he gets them eventually. The witches' magic wears off after a while and they get bored of toying with him. Their about the magical equivalent of a drunken frat house hazing committee, not heartless miscreants like the Banshees."

"Well," Vincent Death said, "we've got nothing to do but wait for the Banshees to show. Want to give this guy a hand?"

The old man ran past with his Marx Brothers precision again. This time he raspberried Vincent and Cowboy Death as he whizzed past.

"Yee haw! Let's wrangle us a greasy pig!" Cowboy Death exclaimed as the *tap, tap, tap* of Salem Death approached again.

This time the other two Deaths joined the pursuit. It sounded like an army drum corps marching down the street as all their bones hit the bricks.

***

Wanda looked over Belladonna's shoulder from the belfry of The Witch House. They were spying the three Deaths on the street below. Wanda could not decide which she loathed more, her husband for trying to live a new life free of her or the pitiful, wrinkled, dusty old mess of a Banshee that Belladonna was. Though the Banshees purported to work independently, it was clear from the start that Belladonna was calling the shots in the Squadron. Wanda only saw her as the woman coming between her and her man, Vincent.

From the moment Belladonna and her Squadron had scooped up Wanda and her soul, Margie, she had felt like the power was taken from her hands. Wanda still felt a burning urge to return Maggie to the boatman on the River Styx, and yet here they were chasing around Death on some crazy quest to start a war. All just to prove that Banshees could not be pushed around.

Fooey to that Wanda thought. She wasn't interested in the war. She was interested in getting back her man under the rule of her iron fist and setting the soul attached to her where it belonged. Yet here she was with Belladonna standing between her and Vincent and for the moment she was helpless to do anything about it. But she was biding her time. She was using these Banshees and waiting for the opportune moment.

Banshees were solitary creatures, and she felt the need to act alone. It was a natural feeling that ran through her cold, congealed blood.

Behind her one of the other Banshees began to murmur. She looked over her shoulder to see Xena shuddering and holding her mummified hands over her mouth. She was fighting back the urge to wail. It was the soul on the street below, she felt its call.

The others in the Squadron tried to calm Xena but she was shaking like a junkie. If she wailed, the squadron's cover would be blown. They would lose the element of surprise. If she couldn't control herself, Belladonna was going to have to give the signal to attack.

Wanda looked back to Belladonna. She was still as a statue. Was she even aware that Xena was about to lose it? Wanda looked out the window and saw the charge on the run from the three Deaths that pursued it. They were running back up the street toward The Witch House. The Squadron needed to spring the attack now. Xena would not hold out long enough for the Charge to get back just under the window where the Squadron could scoop it up before the Deaths could chase it down.

Wanda signaled for the squadron to attack and leapt out the window to lead the charge. The others followed, relieved to be able to wail. Belladonna was the last out the window, frozen for just a moment by Wanda's audacity to lead the charge. She wailed loudest, driven by anger.

***

The Three Witches of Witch House sat on the creaky wooden porch outside Witch House. Their frocks were as black as the clapboard that adorned the house. They all wore pointed black hats as well, though that was for the benefit of the tourists, nobody who lived in Salem needed the benefit of theatricality to know what the women were.

The tallest of the three cackled in a high pitch as she pointed a thick, gnarly stick in the direction of the human she now had under her spell. Sure, it was unethical by most covens' standards to control another living being as such but other covens didn't have the power of mortal seethsaying. The Three Witches of Witch House had the ability to know who around them was poised to move on to the next world. So, as they saw it, this person would be dead already if not for them. And they were only cheating Death by a smidge. After they had their fun, they let Death take its course.

And if Death came for them? Well, they had something special for that as well.

"Come on, Mordrina, I'm bored of this already," the short, rotund witch of the trio spoke out. She rolled her r's like she was choking on gravel, her inflection was masculine.

"Mildeweena, how often do we get to toy with three Deaths? Not very, so hush up and have some fun," Mordrina said, not taking her focus off the person she was controlling with her wand.

"Mordrina's right," Minerva said, "it's a special occasion. The cauldron can wait. It won't boil over." She bounced with as much delight as the bubbles in her voice.

Mordrina led them back up the street. Her powers were not unlike steering a remote controlled car; they would only reach so far before the signal would no longer reach. Though she was having fun taunting Death, she wondered why there were three this time. One Death was as familiar to them as an uncle but the other two were new and the one that looked like a cowboy from the Old West was unsettling.

Mildeweena feared this may mean the Deaths were growing tired of being played with. Had they sent reinforcements? If they didn't let this person go soon, would even more Death come to Salem? It was three on three now but if more came, would they be able to repel them? She wished her sisters would just cut this one loose and lay off the games for a little while. They were bringing too much heat.

Minerva danced around on the porch. She was having fun just because they were having fun. She didn't really care that they were taunting the Deaths. She was just feeding on the positive energy from doing so. "Amuck! Amuck! Amuck!" she sang, and skipped around in a circle. She was imitating her favorite part from her favorite movie, a movie she was sure to go inside to watch again on the television while her sisters boiled down a new potion in the cauldron.

Mildeweena was about to cry out for her obnoxious, younger sister to quit being so bubbly when a dreadful wailing from above did it for her.

The three sisters crouched down, cowering on the porch of The Witch House. A black cloud that cried like a possessed baby whooshed down from above them. The awful cloud raced towards the human the Deaths were chasing.

The sisters watched, stunned, as the cowboy-looking Death retrieved a lasso from inside his robe and twirled it above his head before casting it out at the human. The lasso ringed the human just as the crying black cloud was about to envelop him. The cowboy Death cinched up the lasso and wrangled the human back to him.

The Three Witches of Witch House watched as the black cloud halted its charge and revealed itself to be made of a group of Banshees.

"Hot damn we got us some Banshees too!" Mordrina shouted. She rose to her feet like an excited baseball fan watching a baseball about to sail out of the park for a homerun.

"This can't be good," Mildeweena said, getting back on her feet as well.

"They're cute! Can we keep one?" Minerva said, oblivious the gravity of the situation they were witnessing.

The Deaths and the Banshees were exchanging words but they were too far away to make out what exactly the conversation was. One Banshee, who stood at the head of their group, seemed to be taking exception to one Death in particular who was sort of hanging back apprehensively behind the other two Deaths. The cowboy looking Death held the lassoed human behind him, apparently guarding him from the Banshees. The Death from Salem seemed more concerned with getting his charge from the cowboy Death than he did with the presence of the Banshees.

"Minerva, fetch me the lilac," Mordrina whispered.

Minerva skipped inside The Witch House.

"Are you serious right now?" Mildeweena asked Mordrina.

"Oh yeah. I'll never get an opportunity like this again. Make sure you cast your memory enchantment, we're going to want to remember this for as long as we live!"

"Which may not be all that long considering what you're about to do. If you botch this spell, we are just as dead as that poor soul they've got," Mildeweena said.

Minerva returned with an aerosol can

depicting a blooming lilac bush on a tranquil summer afternoon and handed it to Mordrina.

The argument between the two factions was getting tense. The group of Banshees was inching in closer to the group of Deaths. Their shouting was growing louder and more angered. Mordrina was half tempted to leave them be and witness what an all out physical brawl between Deaths and Banshees would look like.

But that was a bad idea. It wouldn't be good for them, their house or all of Salem for that matter. This plane of existence was not made to bear the burden of a battle between beings not of this world. Mordrina would have to do what was right.

Mordrina held her knobby magic wand up to her face and spoke a few words that would be unrecognizable as language to most humans. Down the street, the man she had been controlling came back under the control of his own devices. He came to as if waking from a dream to find himself in the predicament he was in and soiled himself. The Deaths and Banshees were too far embroiled in their contempt for one another to notice.

Mordrina then let loose several liberal blasts of lilac scented spray onto her wand.

"Nothing like the sweet smell of lilac to get rid of the stench of death and decay," she said in her graveled voice.

She spoke more words unfamiliar to the modern world. Up the street a Banshee grabbed the death that looked like a cowboy. It took less than a moment after that for the other Banshees to pounce. The air began to rumble with the angry cries of enraged Banshees. The hapless soul caught in the middle somehow broke free of the melee and escaped.

Mordrina aimed her wand at the battling death bringers. A swirling focus of soft pink aroma shot from the wand trailing like a bottle rocket and exploded into a cloud of flowers and debris when it hit the battling Deaths and Banshees. They were broken apart and swirled like a tornado, splitting into two vortices. The faster they spun, the fainter they became until both Banshee and Death alike evaporated from existence.

"And that," Mordrina growled, "is how you get rid of death."

Mildeweena huffed, not satisfied that, even though they were safe, they could have been killed.

Minerva bounded and skipped and shouted, "Amuck! Amuck! Amuck! It's time to watch Hocus Pocus again!"

Chapter 8: La Petite Mort

Vincent Death, Cowboy Death and the Death from Salem swirled along the purple highway, the experience ten times more dizzying than their normal journey along the ethereal highway. They were shot back all the way to Headquarters where they came out of the ether like three rotten tomatoes being thrown against a wall. It was fortunate they were no longer made of flesh or they'd be a pool of blood and sinew. Instead, they were a jumble of disconnected bones.

Somewhere in the pile of bones, Vincent Death's jaw bone said, "Fuck this shit! I'm done!"

Cowboy Death's teeth rattled from atop the pile, "What? No! You can't give up, Partner! We're so close!"

From somewhere deep in the pile of bones, the Death from Salem mumbled something too muffled by the jumble of humeri and femurs and metatarsals that lay heaped above him.

"So close? I'm much further than when I started. And it's only my first day on the job. Not only can't I retrieve one simple soul, but I've started a war! I didn't even ask for any of this! I was only doing this for…" Vincent Death held back his last thought.

"Doing it for what? The pay? Ha! There's no salary. What are you doing it for, Death? Not one of us here is doing it out of a sense of obligation.

Fact is, we all started out just like you. This was thrust upon us. But we're all motivated to do it for something. What's your motivation, Death? What's driven you this far on your shittiest day?"

"It's silly."

"Nothing silly about it, partner. Know why I do it?" Cowboy Death's teeth asked. "So I can go back and roam the plains."

"That doesn't sound very exciting," Vincent Death's jawbone said.

"You weren't a cowboy. You wouldn't understand. For me, I'd give anything to go back to the plains. Doing this, this thing we do, it allows me the opportunity to roam the plains from time to time. I'm the Death from Oklahoma. Plus, they let me wear the hat. It gives me a real sense of identity."

"It's the girl," Vincent Death said.

"The girl? Your ex-wife? She's driving you to do this shit? Hell, I don't blame you for bowing out, partner! I'd have thrown myself into limbo right out the gate if I were you!"

"Geeze, thanks," Vincent Death's jawbone said. "Not my ex-wife. The other girl. The one I can't have. Maggie's daughter, Aileen."

"You sly dog you!" Cowboy Death said. "You ain't supposed to fall in love with the living."

"She's everything Wanda never was,"

Vincent Death said and sighed.

"You best get those thoughts out of your mind, partner. There won't be no more loving for you in this life. In case you hadn't noticed, you're made up of bones, all except that particular bone."

"It's not like that at all," Vincent Death protested. "I want to do right by her. I want to get her mother to where she belongs. I wanna give her inner peace. I want to gaze into her eyes even for just one more time."

"Yer one sentimental hombre, I'll give you that. But when this is over you may want to reconsider your motivations. Maybe more healthy drives like bowls of steaming batwing soup or five car pile-ups at stock car races."

Under them, the Death from Salem began muttering something incoherent again. The tone of his mumbling sounded abrupt and worried. Before Vincent Death's jawbone or the collection of Cowboy Death's teeth could try to get clarification, the whole pile of bones began to swirl around and up off the floor like a dust devil born to life.

Vincent Death could feel each piece of himself swirl in the whirlwind. He began to feel whole again as the whipping winds manipulated his bones back into place. It was not long before he was standing on his own two legs and realized he was more than just a jaw bone.

He checked himself physically to be assured

he was all there. He looked next to him and saw Cowboy Death and the Death from Salem also standing there. At least, he assumed it was them. They both looked exactly alike standing there without their Tattered Black Robes™, all skeleton as they day they were reborn. Vincent Death's non-existent heart leaped into the void where his throat once was when he realized he was also naked, naked as Deaths go.

"Put your clothes back on, you perverts!" a voice yelled, and Vincent's vision went black.

The voice was thick with an outrageous French accent, really over-the-top like a Monty Python skit. Vincent Death could not see the owner of the voice because his Tattered Black Robe™ covered his face when it was thrown at him.

Embarrassed, he threw his robe on with the haste of a man caught cheating with someone's wife. He didn't know why he felt ashamed of his bare bones but he felt more like himself with the robe back on. It was easier to distinguish Cowboy and the Death from Salem as well with their robes back on. They all had identities again, without them they were just Death.

"Which one of you is the responsible for this colossal mess?" the French voice asked.

Vincent Death looked around for the source of the voice. He saw nothing.

"I told you he was here," the Death from

Salem said.

"You told us who's here?" Vincent Death asked, still looking around.

"La Petite Mort," the Death from Salem said.

"Say who now?" Vincent Death asked.

"La Petite Mort. He's right there in front of you," the Death from Salem said pointing at Vincent Death's feet.

"Ahh, shit," Cowboy Death said.

Vincent Death looked down. At his feet he saw a Death action figure. Except it wasn't an action figure, it was a tiny fucking Death. It was looking right back up at him and it was fucking pissed.

"You are the piece of shit that has caused all the trouble, oui?" La Petite Mort asked Vincent Death.

"Now, hold on. There maybe a problem but that doesn't give you the right to call me a piece of sh—"

"Fuck you! I will call you what I want when I want. Do you not know who I am? I am La Petite Mort! Death doesn't fuck with me! I fuck with Death!"

La Petite Mort swung his tiny scythe and whacked Vincent Death in the shin. Vincent Death cried out. It was the worst pain he'd ever felt in this life or the previous one. Had he not been blinded by the pain, Vincent Death would have pondered how such a tiny object, swung by such a tiny creature could inflict such enormous pain.

"Enough of your lip-bone Death! I am here to unfuck this for you. Normally we just let you rot in limbo for the rest of your eternities but this case has been deemed exceptional. You've caused a monumental pile of shit."

"You're going to fix this? You're the size of a G.I. Joe doll. There is a squadron of Banshees hell bent on moving in on our territory and they are led by my crazy ex-wife. How, pray tell, are you going to stop them?" Vincent Death asked.

"You need another whack in the shins again, mon ami mort?"

Vincent Death still felt the sting on his shin bone. "Point taken."

"Take up your scythes, gentlemen. We're going back in the assault vehicle."

The Death from Salem tried to offer protest, "Me too? I didn't ask for this. These two boneheads jumped in on my action and fucked it all up."

"You sissy little freak! Call this reconciliation for all those years you've allowed those witches to screw with you," La Petite Mort said.

"Witches?" the Death from Salem asked, confused.

"I rest my case. Let's go!"

The three Deaths followed La Petite Mort down a stony black corridor that led to a corrugated steel garage door.

La Petite Mort reached inside his tiny Tattered Black Robe™ and pulled out a teeny-tiny key fob and aimed it at the garage door. There was a loud electric chirp and then the door clattered and clanged as it opened up.

Vincent Death, Cowboy Death and The Death from Salem all gasped when they saw the vehicle waiting inside.

It was humongous. It shined despite being jet black. The tires alone were taller than any of them. It was trimmed out in green and it looked downright diabolical.

Vincent Death read the name emblazoned on the side of the 1950 panel truck style body, "Grave digger," he said in whispered amazement.

"That's a hell of a steel horse you got there, partner!" Cowboy Death said.

"Does it have seat belts?" The Death from Salem asked.

"She is a beautiful, no?" La Petite Mort said, admiring his ride.

"Beautiful, yes," Vincent Death said. "But can she kill Banshees?"

La Petite Mort took another swipe at Vincent Death with his scythe. Vincent Death hopped over the business end of it, avoiding another stinging strike. This time.

"How dare you question the capabilities of my ride! The Digger and I have rode across these planes of existence and others for many millennia. The cowboy, he is correct, The Digger is my trusty steed."

Chapter 9: Death In A Truck

La Petite Mort revved the engine of the monster truck. The chassis rattled, threatening to come apart. Vincent Death also rattled, threatening to come apart. La Petite Mort let off the throttle and the rumbling eased a bit. Vincent Death was trying to figure out exactly how La Petite Mort was reaching the pedals to rev the engine when he was thrown back into his seat as the truck took off at a speed he was not prepared for.

"We're driving straight for the wall!" Vincent Death shouted out over the scream of the truck's engine.

"Don't worry, mon ami mort! The Grave Digger, she's equipped with the flux capacitor, no?" La Petite Mort shouted back.

The little Death was as calm as a cucumber as the truck rocketed toward the solid rock wall. Vincent Death was not ready to accept the reality of a flux capacitor when it kicked into gear as Grave Digger hit exactly 88 mph. The monster truck illuminated in a flash of lightening and found its way onto the inter-dimensional highway along which the Death's travel.

Much like flying solo, Vincent Death felt the disorienting feeling of traveling along the ether.

He'd traveled enough now that it was not a vomit inducing experience, but being seated in the vehicle renewed his queasiness.

Before Vincent Death had a chance to ask where they were headed, the truck flashed off the purple plasma highway and the Deaths found themselves mid-air over a dirt track hovering just above a line of junk cars all painted a sickening shade of sky blue. It didn't take longer than a moment for the truck to lose momentum and fall to the ground, smashing the cars underneath. The truck bounced off them like a rubber ball and bounded into the air for a moment more, bounding like a frog onto a few more cars down the line.

The monster truck drove off the lineup of junk cars, and there was a deafening roar. All the Deaths covered the ears they would have had were they not skeletons. La Petite Mort grabbed a safety helmet out of the glove compartment and put it on his head. He climbed out the window of the truck onto the roof. The roar elevated another octave. The air vibrated and Vincent Death thought they had driven into the lair of a giant monster about to devour them.

He winced, expecting the truck to be eaten in one swallow. But it never came and Vincent Death began to look around and realize they were sitting in a large arena, and the roar wasn't an angry monster but the accolades of an appreciative audience.

"This little guy is going to get us killed,"

Vincent Death said.

"No can do, Partner," Cowboy Death said. "We're already dead. You ain't been studying that book at all, have you?"

"When have I had even a moment of time to open up the book to study?" Vincent Death yelled over the wild applause of the crowd.

"Please don't tell me this is his first charge we're chasing after," the Death from Salem begged.

"Ah-yep," Cowboy Death said in the affirmative.

"I fucking hate you guys. I really do," the Death from Salem said.

La Petite Mort climbed back in the cab. He pulled off his helmet. He wore a smile bigger than his diminutive stature. Vincent Death could tell La Petite Mort was in his happy place. A miniscule Death who enjoyed driving monster trucks. It was the afterlife equivalent of a guy with a small penis driving a Corvette. There was a lot to compensate for when you were that small.

From behind them, they heard an engine turn over and roar to life. The cab of Grave Digger suddenly brightened. The four Deaths looked over their shoulder out the back of the truck and winced at the bright headlights glaring into their truck. Another monster truck had roared to life and revved with a palpable fury. The engine screamed and smoke exploded from the other truck's exhaust pipes as it accelerated in their direction.

The other truck zipped up a dirt ramp just in front of the line of junked and smashed cars and went airborne. La Petite Mort fired up Grave Digger in a flash, trying to get out of the path of the psycho monster truck on a collision course with them. Vincent Death's cold, dusty heart sank when he heard melancholy wailing over the growl of the monster truck soaring toward them. The Banshees had a monster truck of their own.

La Petite Mort had Grave Digger back to life but the Banshees' monster was already bearing down on them. The nose of the Banshees' truck slammed into Grave Digger and launched the monster truck forward. The force of the collision whipped the Death from Salem's head so hard it rolled off his neck bones and onto the the floor.

"This is fucking bullshit," the Death from Salem said reaching for his skull, but being held back by the seatbelt.

The crowd went ape shit crazy. Never before had they witnessed a demolition derby of monster trucks. Vincent Death wasn't thrilled being part of history. La Peitite Mort got on the accelerator again and Grave Digger lurched forward of it own volition. The damage they had taken from the initial impact had been cosmetic at worst.

"They've got their own monster truck too? Let's get the fuck out of here!" Vincent Death yelled.

"Like Hell we're getting out of here, mon ami! Nobody messes with the the truck of La Petite Mort and gets away with it!" the tiny Death said.

"He's right pardner!" Cowboy Death said, hanging onto his Stetson. "We need to have us a showdown! Yeee haa!"

The Death from Salem just kept repeating, "I want to go home," over and over again, holding tight to his skull in his lap.

La Petite Mort circled Grave Digger around trying to turn back on the Banshees' monster truck. The Banshees matched the maneuver and the two trucks circled around the arena floor, a cat chasing its tail.

La Petite Mort sped the truck up. Then, without warning, he slammed on the brakes. Grave Digger stopped short so fast, the rear end lifted up off the ground, the truck going into a handstand on its front tires.

The Banshee's truck, not prepared for La Petite Mort's unexpected maneuver, drove under Grave Digger and plowed into the undercarriage of its front end. The force of the impact dropped Grave Digger back on all four tires sitting on top of the Banshees' monster truck.

The Banshees cried out in anger below them. It would have sent the audience into tears if they heard the cry but the crowd roared their approval at the monster truck stunt spectacle they were witnessing. They had saved themselves from unexplained grief without realizing it.

La Petite Mort shifted Grave Digger into reverse and slammed on the gas. Vincent Death still wasn't sure how he was reaching the pedals and at the moment he didn't much care. Grave Digger rolled off the top of the Banshees' monster truck, leaving a bad ass set of burnt rubber tracks on the roof. Grave Digger shot forward and smashed into the rear of the other truck. If the Banshees cried louder, out of frustration and anger, the Deaths couldn't hear it over the growing roar of the crowd. This was not your everyday, run-of-the-mill monster truck rally.

La Petite Mort backed off the crippled rear end of the nemesis vehicle. Then, he shot through the gears, increasing speed as he maneuvered toward one of the dirt ramps built up on the arena floor. Like a seasoned professional wrestler, Grave Digger went airborne and landed square on the Banshees' truck. Jimmy "Superfly" Snooka would have been proud.

The force of Grave Digger landing on top of the Banshees' truck crushed the cab down on their vehicle, the roll cage unable to withstand that type of impact. La Petite Mort shifted gears but found Grave Digger was hung up on the wreck underneath them. The engine screamed in vain. It was the only sound in the arena now.

The crowd had loved seeing the duel of the trucks. They were in stunned silence now as they realized collectively that whoever was in the truck Grave Digger had landed on could not have survived. It was all fun and games until a monster truck landed on your head.

***

One of the benefits of being a Banshee is that you cannot die when a monster truck lands on your head. Instead, the squadron of Banshees pinned inside the flattened cab had squirmed like worms out any orifice they could seek out on the floor of the truck. They scattered from the wreck like a murder of crows flapping away to their next omen.

Wanda wailed, frustrated. Her husband and his stupid friends had turned the tables on them. She fucking hated when he got one up on her. She wanted to make him pay but felt she could not squeeze one more ounce of fury into her soul.

She realized she couldn't hear herself think over the scream of the engine once she freed herself from the truck. That's when she realized that her husband and his friends had made a fatal mistake. They thought they had trapped her squadron of Banshees when in fact it was the Deaths who were trapped.

She signaled the swarming Banshees to go for the truck. They bunched into formation and swooped at the open window of the truck. Four Deaths and seven Banshees wrestled, rolled, rocked and brawled inside the cramped quarters of the truck.

When the ruckus had ended, the Banshees flew out of the confines of the truck. Captured Deaths raised aloft as their victory trophy in the battle of monster trucks.

The crowd who had just witnessed the greatest monster truck rally in the history of motor sports all made their way for the exits. They were crying their eyes out. They had no idea why. To them, it felt like someone had just died.

Chapter 10: Death Becomes Her

Vincent Death crawled out from under the passenger seat of Grave Digger. The only sound he could hear in the entire arena was the soft grumble of the monster truck's engine idling. He found the kill switch on the dashboard and engaged it. Grave Digger's motor died.

They were all gone. La Petite Mort, The Death from Salem and Cowboy Death, all gone. The Banshees were gone also. The spectators who had been treated to the greatest spectacle they would ever witness in their living lives, gone as well, not a single straggler left behind.

Just Vincent Death.

He felt like he'd lived a lifetime as the Grim Reaper. He realized it hasn't even been a full day. He also realized his day must be running out. That meant his first day would also be his last. The Banshees had won. His ex-wife, Wanda, had ruined his life again. There was no escaping her, even in death.

He resigned himself to going back to the Tennessee office of the League of Deaths and admitting to his failure. He just needed to do one last thing before being cast off to limbo or worse, have his soul erased.

He needed to see Aileen one last time.

He climbed down the enormous tire of the monster truck and placed his skeletal feet into the soft dirt on the monster truck track. He tapped his scythe and shimmered out of the arena.

Death knocked on Aileen O'Kelly's door and she answered. Death was here for her but this time not for the usual reason. Her heart filled with hope when she saw Vincent Death standing on her doorstep. She was overjoyed that he was there to let her know her mother was delivered safely to the other side as promised. She was filled with dread when Death told her her mother's soul had been kidnapped by Banshees and he was unable to get her to the other side.

"You're telling me a war between the escorts of the dead has broken out over my mother?" Aileen asked.

Vincent Death twiddled his fingers, not looking directly at Aileen. "You make it sound so epochal but, yeah, that's about the size of it."

"I love my sainted mother!" Aileen cried out in a thick brogue. "I love her very much and I hate that she has to die but this is not what was meant for her. You said you would fix this. You promised me. Now you're here telling me that all hope is lost. Why are you doing this to me? I thought you cared about me! I could see it in your eyes. I believed in you, Death."

"Vincent," Vincent Death corrected.

"Huh?"

"Vincent is my name. Well, Vincent Death, I suppose."

"You have a name?" Aileen asked, bewildered.

"Yeah, I guess so. I never really thought about it. Everyone has just been calling me Death. But nobody said I couldn't have a name so, yeah, Vincent Death is my name."

"Well okay then, Mr. Vincent Death. You lost my mother and I hate you and now I have a name to attach to that hate."

Vincent Death felt smaller than La Petite Mort. He did make grand promises to Aileen having no idea if he was capable of living up to them. Aileen had set his heart aflutter and he wanted to tell her anything she wanted to hear just to find a reason to see her again.

"Oh Aileen! I'm so sorry. I can't begin to tell you how devastated I am with myself. I made promises to you I could not keep. I'm new at this, this is my first day on the job as a matter of fact. And you, I was so stricken by your emerald eyes and angelic voice, I would have promised you the moon if it meant the opportunity for you to ask me to bring it to you if only to see you once more. You affect the heart that I no longer have.

"I would bring you with me if I could. I bet your mother would cross to the other side for that

[123]

same chance to see you one last time. As Death, I can feel her soul and her soul is distressed that it was taken away before she could bid you a final goodbye."

"So take me with you," Aileen said, upset that Death did not offer in the first place.

"Taking you with me would mean you would have to die also. And if you die before your time…"

Vincent Death's empty, black eye sockets went cartoon wide.

"And if I die before my time, what?" Aileen said, waiting for Vincent Death to finish.

"And you become as me!" he exclaimed. "You become Death as I am! You could come back with me and see your mother one last time and see her off on her journey across the Styx and then you and I could be—"

"Together," Aileen said, finishing for Vincent Death this time.

Butterflies exploded from his chest hearing her say the words. Maybe they were moths, they always looked the same to Vincent. He turned to her, his smile as big as a skeleton without flesh could smile, which is pretty fucking big when it was unencumbered by lips and cheeks and chins and cheeks. Nothing but teeth.

Aileen grasped Vincent Death's hands and pulled him close to her and said, "Kill me."

***

"What happens when you kill Death?" Wanda asked the rest of the squadron.

"Same as us, they are erased *forever*," one of the squadron replied with a lingering cry on the last word.

"Excellent. But let's not kill them yet," Wanda said, tracing her wrinkled finger along The Death from Salem's cheek bone.

"Why not?" another Banshee from the squadron whimpered. "One less Death we have to deal with, and having two of them captive is too risky as it is."

"We need them as bait," Wanda said.

"To lure in the other Death that was with them?"

"No, bait for the ferryman. We're really going to fuck shit up now. We're going to get Charon on the payroll and if he won't play our game then we'll just have to take him out as well."

"Now you're talking!" cried the former leader of the squad. She still resented Charon for turning their stolen sole away. He was responsible for this whole mess.

"Gather up this rabble!" Wanda commanded. "We're headed back to the Styx!"

The Banshees cried and took flight. They scooped up Maria, La Petite Mort, Cowboy Death and The Death from Salem and thundered like a black tornado toward the River Styx.

***

Death speared Aileen O'Kelly through the head with a creosote crusted fire poker. She fell to the floor, dead. Blood spilled out of the large hole in her head like a decorative fountain, pooling around her, creating a gruesome crime scene for some overachieving young detective that would find her body the next day. Death felt tears of joy well up inside his empty body. He had killed the woman he loved.

Now the only thing left to do was to be sure no other Deaths came to try to claim her. He was fairly certain that would not be a problem. As far as he knew, Deaths worked in territories and this murder occurred on his turf. Aileen would be his charge anyway. It would only be a matter of time before she rose up and became Death as he had back in Tijuana.

Vincent Death had no way of telling how long his body had been baking out in the fiery Tijuana sun before he rose as Death. He felt like he needed a drink and rummaged through Aileen's bar. Vincent Death was pleased that Aileen lived up to the stereotype of the Irish and found the bar was loaded with alcohol, with a definite inclination for whiskey. He poured himself a shot and threw it back. It burned going down and soaked his Tattered Black Robe™ on the other end of his chest. It was a bitch not having flesh but at least there was some sensation still involved with imbibing alcohol.

Vincent Death began pacing the house. There was no sense continuing to drink even if it wouldn't get him inebriated it was still going to make his Tatter Black Robe™ wet and clingy and just as uncomfortable as soaked underwear. He circled around the house until he wound up back at Aileen's corpse. He waded into the pool of blood she lay in. He gazed down at her, into her dead emerald eyes. It was easier looking into those enraptured eyes when they lacked the soul behind them. There were no less beautiful, though. He hoped beyond hope that somehow she would retain those hypnotic green eyes in Death. He wasn't sure how since no Death he had met had anything less than empty, black eye sockets, but he hoped with the naiveté of a child that her special eyes would be the exception to the rule.

He stared down at her, into her, through her and back at himself. He stared for so long he lost track of how long he had been standing there looking at her. Seeing a future with her, wondering what a past with her would have been like instead of Wanda. He'd daydreamed a life yet to be lived with her in Death. How long had he been standing there? Hours? Days?

Vincent Death drew his attention back to Aileen's corpse. Did he detect a twitch from his periphery? His ashen heart leapt into his throat with the hope that his bride-to-be had come back to him in death.

He knelt down at her side, dipping his knee in her coagulating blood. Vincent Death meant to comfort Aileen so she would not be so startled to wake up as a grim reaper. He knew she was expecting it but couldn't be sure how much she would remember in the transformation.

Aileen exploded off the floor like a bomb. Her gray, wrinkled face stopped microns from Vincent Death's skull. She cried in horror into his face, shoved him away from her and then she took flight out the door and off into the dark sky.

It never occurred to Vincent Death that his beloved Aileen could become a Banshee. He only thought of Banshees as awful things like his ex-wife and her rabble. How could he have been so stupid? That was it. There was nothing left for him.

He stood up and tapped his scythe to the wood floor. He shimmered out of sight. He slid along the ethereal highway to the Styx where he would allow Wanda and the other Banshees to tear him apart. He would allow them to take out all their hate and anger and aggression on him.

He was far too afraid to face failure as a Death among his peers. That seemed like a worse fate.

Chapter 11: Death on the Styx

Death sat behind his worn out desk. The wood was so old it was gray and splitting along the ancient grains. Unfathomable piles of paper were stacked haphazard upon the desk's warped surface. There was just enough space among the mess for Death to review the day's manifest.

He traced his pointy finger down the names on the list, being sure each name had been checked in and accounted for on the day. The task was monotonous. Death had been doing the job so long he did not know how to do anything else, including bringing souls to the other side himself. He was a Death who could not bring death. He was a Death accountant, The Grim Bean Counter.

His routine never changed. He began his review of the day's manifest at the exact same moment day after day. He never mixed up his approach. He stayed with the A's and worked his way to the Z's, day in and day out. He was careful and attentive. Not one name or check slipped past his glance.

So as he did every day for an uncountable number of eternities, he started at A. There was an Abercrombie and an Abernathie. There were several Allens, a handful more Allins. There were two Allains. On and on, he ran down the list, Ajax,

Appleby, Armani, right down through Azerbaijani.

He moved onto the B's without skipping a beat. So far, all souls had been accounted for.

***

The squadron of Banshees swept in low over the River Styx. An awful screeching accompanied their approach as they bared down on the boat landing. The black swirling cloud of Banshees aimed for the torches at the dock where Charon's skiff made port.

For all their dark and nefarious theatrics, not a soul was around to be intimidated by their arrival. Wanda and the rest of the squadron looked up and down the river for the Boatman but not a vessel crept along the blood red waters of the Styx.

Cowboy Death, La Petite Mort and the Death from Salem both struggled to break free of the grasp of their captors. The Banshees holding them were as strong as iron shackles. Maria did not struggle or complain. She was tired and just wanted to cross the River Styx to the Other Side and get on with her life after death. Still, she longed for one final goodbye to her daughter, Aileen.

The squadron cried as one, angry and upset that Charon was not here waiting for them. Their cries upset Wanda further. She squealed like a thing dying. That only served to incite the rest of the squadron into further dramatic cries. Wanda grew more frustrated with their bitching and squealed even louder. They sounded worse than a pack of wolves howling in the night.

Still, the boatman didn't appear. Off in the distance, approaching the boatman's landing, someone else did appear: a tiny shadow that grew bigger as it approached.

***

Vincent Death followed some sense of instinct as he trudged his way towards Charon's dock. He was distraught and lost within his own empty mind. He knew his afterlife was over. There was no way he could get himself out of this colossal fuck up. He could have just sat down and waited on the steps of Aileen's house. Done nothing until whatever it was that would come for him and do whatever it was they did with Deaths who couldn't do their job. He was never offered specifics but by all vague accounts, it didn't sound pleasant or quick.

He trudged on, getting closer to the Styx with each meager step.

He could have opened the book while he waited for his fate on Aileen's front step. He was pretty sure the book would give him a clear and concise answer as to what terrible thing awaited him. In fact, he realized, he could have consulted the book at any point and time during this day to get a good answer. Instead, he waited out his final end because he shot from the hip at every step. He relied on those around him who, even if they had the best of intentions, only seemed to lead him further astray.

He walked up to Charon's landing on the Styx. There, he found his friends and his charge being held by a squadron of banshees and his ex wife. They all looked at him like he was fucking crazy. That was good, because he was. He waved hello to them and stood there as if they were all there waiting on a bus.

***

"Kill him!" Wanda shrieked.

The squadron pounced like sprung jack-in-the-boxes. The ones holding prisoners stood their ground. Vincent Death didn't try to fight, he just stood there, unflinching as the Banshees pounced upon him.

He was punched in the knees. He was pelted in the ribs. At one point, a Banshee kicked him in the jaw. His jaw fell to the ground and he bent over and picked it up, putting it back in place as the Banshees beat him like they were in a high school pile on.

Vincent Death resigned himself to his fate. The beating he was taking wasn't all that bad, really. It was more obnoxious than anything. There wasn't anything that he could categorize as pain involved. He was almost sorry he hadn't taken on the Banshees sooner.

The Banshees tried in vain to rip Vincent Death limb from limb, but he would just pick himself up and put himself back together. They were tiring of the exercise in futility. They beat on him, more afraid of what Wanda might do to them if they stopped than they were afraid that Death wasn't what they could call, conquerable.

"Why won't you die?" Wanda cried out in anger.

The indifference in Vincent Death was washed away by a wave of absolute frustration with his ex-wife. She didn't fucking get it. All this shit, all this turmoil and chaos, it all came back to her. And not just since she started fucking with him as a Banshee but before that. This ball was set rolling right from their Earthly marriage. She was a nag. She was self-centered and didn't have an ounce of care how Vincent ever felt. Not once, not never. It was always only about Wanda. She just never, ever got that. Right up to this very moment, she didn't get it.

He opened his mouth to tell her she had no idea what she was doing; that was why he wasn't dying. He wanted to throw it in her face that all that bad shit that happened to her in her life that she blamed squarely on him was at its core her fault because she was incapable of thinking beyond herself. Instead, he opened his mouth and his jaw became dislodged, falling to the ground once more; this time the bone shattered and split in two.

Had he had tear ducts he would have shed a tear. That tear would have snowballed into a river of emotional release and the tears would have become a full out bawling. He would have cried aloud so deep and long that it would have made every one of the Banshees jealous how awful his crying would have sounded. He saw his shattered jawbone on the rocky ground and he knew he was free.

If he could not die, he could just crumble into a million pieces and be forgotten in this forsaken land as so much dust. He cast off his Tattered Black Robe™ which fell to the ground with a thump, weighed down by the Book he had stowed away inside all this time. He cast his arms out and invited a beating that would obliterate his bones into scattered pieces. He hoped the Banshees would stomp him into a fine powder.

But then the beatings stopped as a new cry echoed across the barren tundra and honed in on the beating taking place on the Styx. Everyone turned in the direction of the cry and saw what appeared to be another Banshee bearing down on them all.

It was Aileen! Or the Banshee formerly known as Aileen.

Vincent Death cursed. The Banshees had not beaten him to a pulp soon enough. Now he would have to deal with, not only his ex-wife and her friends trying to kill him, but the one woman he finally found love for in his cold, dead heart.

***

The Grim Bean Counter continued down his list, the same way he did for the past six eternities. Every entry he scanned was accounted for, the same way they'd be for nearly as long. He had impeccable focus on mundane tasks. It was the very trait that landed him the job. The Grim Bean Counter found his thoughts wandering though. After so long he wanted to find just one entry not accounted for at the end of the day. His mind got excited considering the ability to be able to send a Death to his death.

And then it happened. An entry, unchecked: Maggie O'Kelly. The Grim Bean Counter would have wet himself had his bladder not been a shriveled, hard, morsel of its once glorious form. His finger, that had guided him through daily checklist after daily checklist vibrated with excitement. He grew nervous and panicked. Finally, a soul had gone unaccounted for. It had been an eon at least since he received updated training on the policies and procedures for just such a case.

The Grim Bean Counter did the only thing he could think to do. He jumped up and yelled at the top of his lungs, "We've got one!"

His voice echoed in his small, empty office. Nobody responded. He wasn't shocked. He had no idea what to do but he knew where he had to go. He gathered up his checklist and long unused Scythe and ran out of his office and down the never ending corridor of headquarters toward a door he knew was marked "Limbo".

He entered the office and was greeted in the reception area by a baby with a big head.

"Welcome to Limbo, how can I assist you today?" the giant-headed baby asked.

"I'm not exactly sure on protocol here but I have a Death that needs to be dealt with. He hasn't turned in his charge for the day," the Grim Bean Counter said.

"Oh no, that's terrible news. Have a seat, Mr. Death and I'll page Mr. Limbus immediately."

Another baby with a ridiculously sized cranium approached The Grim Bean Counter after a time and introduced himself as Mr. Limbus. Mr. Limbus appeared to have a full diaper and yet did not seem troubled by this at all. He was nothing short of understanding and professional while The Grim Bean Counter explained the situation he had on his hands.

"Not a problem, Mr. Death, not a problem at all. I will send out my best agent and have this situation resolved with haste! Now, I'll just need you to fill out some forms and wait here while our agent conducts his operation. It won't be but a few more moments."

The Grim Bean Counter sighed. He was going to be stuck in Limbo for awhile.

***

"Oh! Isn't this rich? Your new squeeze is one of us now!" Wanda said. She never sounded more irritating to Vincent Death's ears. "You sure do know how to piss 'em off don't you Vincent?

"It's okay, sweetie. Join the club," Wanda said, putting a friendly arm around Aileen. "We wanna kill him too. He's a no good, rotten, man who won't listen. Ever!"

Aileen kept a blank stare. Vincent assumed she had not fully adjusted to the new thing he had transformed her into. She didn't attempt to squirm away from the friendly embrace Wanda gave her either. She was definitely pissed at him by his estimation.

Join the club, indeed, Vincent Death thought to himself.

"Go on chickie, have a whack at him. Maybe you've got the right touch to finish him off," Wanda invited.

Aileen continued her blank stare. She hadn't spoken a word and Vincent Death hoped it would stay that way. If he heard her mournful Banshee cry, his image of her would be ruined forever. His ears could not stand to hear someone so beautiful sound so sad.

Aileen sauntered over to where Vincent Death stood. She looked so unhappy to him, which made him feel miserable as well. Aileen looked deep into his dark, empty eye sockets, the last vestiges of moisture still trapped inside Vincent

Death's old dead bones threatened to coalesce and form into a tear that he needed to cry.

Aileen reared back with her fist. Vincent Death braced himself. Whether she killed him or not, the pain she was about to inflict would be unbearable. He would be deader than Death for certain. But Aileen winked at him just before she let her fist fly. Vincent Death's eye sockets rose in surprise.

Aileen spun on her heels that floated just inches off the rocky bank of the Styx. Her fist flew forward when she turned 180 degrees and faced the squadron of Wanda and her Banshees.

She stood too far from them to land the punch, but a red, angry blast of molten hatred exploded from her fist and slammed into the squadron like a bowling ball smashing into a set of pins.

Banshees flew in all directions, and a hot ball of nasty energy expanded outward.

Aileen motioned to Vincent Death to cover his skull where his ears would have been. He did as she silently instructed. He blinked her eyes tightly shut. Vincent Death took her cue and also closed his eye sockets shut tight.

Aileen dashed to where two of the Banshees lay in shock. She grabbed each by their throat, choking them off and rendering them silent. She opened her mouth and and cried the most awful cry ever moaned by any being of any sort on any plane of existence. Both Banshees heads exploded, their molecular make-up unable to withstand such a mournful vibration. Aileen repeated the process with the other Banshees who were all stunned from the blast.

Aileen got to Wanda last. She held her up by her neck to cut off her moan as she did the others. Wanda put up more of a fight than the others. She struggled, she squirmed, she wheezed through Aileen's crushing grip. Aileen became more and more annoyed that Wanda was unable to accept the inevitable fate. Wanda would not stop no matter how tightly Aileen gripped her throat. She understood now the torture and annoyance she had caused Vincent in all his life and throughout his short death.

And for that Aileen found no love or remorse in her heart; she only felt empty blackness. The most awful cry let lose from within her and she watched as Wanda's being vibrated out of being and into a puff of dust that settled to the rocky ground on the bank of the River Styx.

A wind kicked up and blew Wanda's ashes across the barren land. The ashes flew toward where Charon's skiff had just docked. Charon breathed them in and launched into a violent coughing fit. He was doubled over his staff and unable to control his gagging.

Vincent Death, Aileen, Cowboy Death, La Petite Mort, the Death from Salem and Aileen's mother all gathered around Charon. Maria reached into her purse and pulled out a lozenge and offered it to Charon.

Charon reached for the lozenge like it was the purest form on oxygen and popped it into his mouth. His coughing subsided without haste. He stood upright, aflush and tearing which was an indicator just how awful he was a moment ago considering he was made of wicker.

"Ohh, thank you so much," Charon said to Maria.

He explained that his throat had been dry for eons. He was frustrated, all he wanted was a hard candy or drop he could suck on to relieve his dry larynx. But everyone kept giving him baubles and treasures and knick-knacks thinking that he was charging a fee to bring the souls to The Other Side. Turns out he does that for free he was just unable to communicate his dire need for something to wet the back of his throat.

Charon felt a reward was in order for finally relieving him of his burden. Maria said there wasn't much reward he could bestow upon her since the completion of her journey to the other side was all the reward she would ever need, and she was getting that anyway. Charon thought about it and found the answer in love.

It was not difficult to sense the deep love that Vincent Death felt for Aileen. He could also tell that Aileen was hard pressed to take her adoring eyes off her beloved Vincent Death. Since Banshees and Deaths mix like water and oil,

Charon felt it was within the scope of his powers to make love right under these extraordinary circumstances. And he would do it for Maria who had freed him from his unwanted muteness.

So Charon decreed that Aileen would be the first Death Banshee known on this plane of existence. Though physically she would remain a Banshee, she would conduct herself as a Death and do as all Deaths did and ushers the souls from that side to this. And thus, Vincent Death and Aileen Death would be together, forever. And ever. And ever.

And ever.

And ever.

The Deaths were huddled around one another, celebrating their victory. Their defeat of the Banshee Squadron was bigger than they could appreciate, and the magnitude of what they had gone through was just beginning to set in. There were hugs, dry tears and plenty of "I love you, mans" to go around. The moment was starting to get uncomfortable with none of them knowing how to move on with their lives from here.

"Who among you is Death?" came a stern voice.

Vincent Death broke from the huddle to come face to face with a man-sized baby. His head was enormous. He spoke like Arnold Schwarzenegger without an Austrian accent which probably made him Lou Ferrigno.

"What the hell are you?!" Vincent Death demanded.

"I'm an agent of Limbo come to detain Death for failure to serve the League of Deaths with regard to preordained duties. Are you Death?"

"I am Death," Vincent Death said.

"Then you're coming with me!"

"But he's Death, too," Vincent Death said pointing to Cowboy Death. "And him, and him and that little thing is Death also. And that fiery looking red-headed one, she's Death too now, I'm told."

Vincent Death blew a kiss to Aileen. She grabbed it out of the air and placed it on her curled up lips.

"Then you are all coming with me! You are to be detained in Limbo forever!"

The giant headed man-baby grabbed Vincent Death by his wrist. Vincent pulled away and stepped back. The other Deaths moved in closer. The giant headed man baby became agitated. He pursed his lips and began to shudder, holding his breath and turning red, then blue in the face. He was having a tantrum. It was almost adorable until his skin started steaming.

"What do we do now, Partner?" Cowboy Death asked.

"Let's put him in time out!" Vincent Death

said.

"Yee-ha!" Cowboy Death yelped.

An upbeat action sequence music score began to play. They all paused and looked at the Death from Salem who was holding a boom box over his head like he was John Cusack in Say Anything. He shrugged and said it felt like the right moment.

Cowboy Death dug out a lasso from his Tattered Black Duster® and began whirling the loop over his head. La Petite Mort produced a tiny phallic shaped vibrating object from within his robe. It was adorable and they all chuckled a bit. La Petite Mort was not impressed.

Vincent Death searched his robe hoping to produce a weapon. He felt the book and almost took it out, but felt something else instead. He whipped it out. It was the roll of duct tape that the Midget Death had given him at the bar. Score, duct tape fixes everything!

The Deaths pounded on the giant headed man baby. La Petite Mort shoved the vibrator into his armpit and the man baby laughed and spasmed uncontrollably. They gave Cowboy Death the opening to slip the lasso around the man baby and cinch it up. Vincent Death hopped in and wrapped the man baby up with the entire role of duct tape.

The giant headed man baby cried and cried.

"I finished my job. My charge is safely to the other side of the Styx. You're a bad baby. Now you sit here and think about what you did!" Vincent Death told the giant headed man-baby.

Aileen ran up to Vincent Death and embraced him. "Oh hunny, you're going to be so good with our children!"

"Children?!" Vincent Death asked, his voice cracking.

The other Deaths laughed and laughed as they all shimmered into the purple plasma highway and back to the office.

Epilogue: Life After Death

Vincent Death held Aileen Death-Banshee's hand as they traveled through the purple plasma on their way to retrieve their latest charge. It was unusual for Deaths to be paired together, in fact, outside of Vincent and Aileen Death-Banshee it had never been done before. Sure, Deaths had teamed up on the job just as Vincent Death did with Cowboy Death and the Death from Salem, but they were never sent out or assigned as a team. But the folks down at HQ just thought Vincent Death and Aileen Death-Banshee worked best as a pairing, each making up for each other's short falls. And they were just so gosh darn cute together.

They shimmered into existence on the human plane and set out to find their charge for the day. There were in a seedy looking alley littered with empty tequila bottles, half eaten churros and blown apart remains of piñatas. Vincent Death's breath caught in his neck bones. Were they back in Tijuana? Though his experience in Tijuana led him here in this place working side by side with the love of his death, Tijuana brought back memories of his ex-wife and their final trip together.

He raised his scythe to tap them out of Tijuana with haste but Aileen Death-Banshee held his arm before he could complete the motion.

"No, wait hunny," Aileen Death-Banshee said. "I don't think this is what you think it is."

She pointed down the alley. What looked like the street at the end began to roll off to the right. The scene was replaced with a row of golf carts lined in a row and there were two security guards enjoying a cup of coffee and talking about anything but whatever it was they were guarding.

They were on a movie lot.

Vincent Death followed the vibrations from his scythe. It led him to a building down at the opposite end of the alley. He opened the door and motioned for his bride to lead the way in. Vincent Death stepped in behind her. He wasn't ready for what he saw.

The entire inside of the building was Heaven. It was giant and open. It was a brilliant, blinding white all around. The pillowy white light was only broken by a single figure standing across the room. The figure was dressed in classy white suit offset by black shoes. The suit was casual, almost island chic but designed by Versace or Armani for certain.

They had found their charge.

With a snap of his fingers Vincent Death and Aileen Death-Banshee found themselves transported across the room and face to face with their charge without taking a single step.

"How did you do that?" Vincent Death asked

the well dressed man.

"I'm God," the well dressed man replied.

"God? But you're our charge. We are here to take you to the other side. Your time has come," Vincent Death said.

God laughed. It was a jovial laugh. It took Vincent Death off guard. He would have figured God would laugh with contempt at the idea of dying.

"He's not God, hunny."

"Well of course I'm God," God said, smiling at the couple.

A tidal wave of water rushed at them from behind God and vanished into the pristine white floor before it washed them all away. God proved his point.

Vincent Death would have pissed himself had he still had a bladder. Now he wasn't sure what they were going to do about the situation. Could God die? And if he could, did Vincent Death have enough gumption to bring him across? And was he willing to allow his wife to take responsibility for killing God if it turned out to be an error on The League of Deaths part?

Everything had gone smooth since the whole debacle with Aileen's mother. They never missed a charge, not even close ever since then. They were even chosen as the Death of the Month for two consecutive months not long ago. It was nice. They got to pick their charges for the day and even had a primo parking space out in front of the office. Of course, they didn't have a car or drive to work but the perk was nice. Vincent Death had even considered bringing back the Monster Truck to park in the spot but figured that would cause more trouble than it was worth.

"Of course he's God! A tidal wave, baby? Only God can produce a tidal wave on demand!"

God nodded. "There, you see," he gave two thumbs up and then pointed them back at himself, "God!"

Aileen Death-Banshee rubbed Vincent Death's chest, cooing to him. "Hunny, think about it? Does God have a name? Is God's name Morgan Freeman?"

"Who's Morgan Freeman?!" God asked.

"Cut!" A voice echoed from somewhere in the vast white room.

Vincent Death whirled sounds on his heels so fast his Tattered Black Robe™ flared out like he was Julie Andrews in The Sound of Music. He was shocked to notice there was an entire film crew behind them watching everything. Had they been there before?

"Morgan, I know you're God but that's not your line!"

"I'm not Morgan! I'm God! Why won't you listen?" Morgan Freeman asked.

"I know you like to stay in character

Morgan, but we're not rolling film," the man said. "I'm the director of this film and I'll decide when it's time for you to act. So please stop. You're starting to freak me out a little bit."

The director walked right up to Vincent Death but looked through him. The man didn't see Death standing right in front of him, he wasn't ready to die.

"I'm not ready to die! I'm God."

"No, you're not going to die. There's too much money riding on this movie for you to die. Once the studio makes bank on Bruce Almighty 3: God Almighty, then you can die all you'd like. But for now I'd simply like you to keep your sanity so we can finish up this film in an orderly fashion. Okay?"

"I'm afraid it is your time, Morgan," Aileen Death-Banshee said, offering him her cold, dead hand.

Morgan Freeman looked at Aileen Death-Banshee's hand. He glanced to the director, then back to Death's hand. In that moment, Morgan Freeman accepted his own Death. But he was going to go out as only Morgan Freeman could.

"Okay. Say, can we test my powers one last time?" Morgan Freeman asked the director.

"The water tanks haven't refilled on the tidal wave machine," the director said.

"No, not that power. The flying rig. The one you use so I can ascend into Heaven in the final scene."

"It's not time to shoot the final scene, Morgan."

"Please, I promise it'll be worth it."

The director rolled his eyes. They were over budget and behind on time already. If Morgan Freeman wanted to shoot the final scene, then he would if it meant getting this movie wrapped so he could get to work on the film that really mattered to him. His swan song, Sharknado 7.

***

"Bruce Almighty 3: God Almighty, ascension scene take one!" the director cried out. "Action!"

"Action?" Vincent Death asked Aileen Death-Banshee. "Don't I have to go to wardrobe or makeup first? Isn't there going to be a read through? Don't these people block scenes out first?"

"They've already done all that! We're not part of this movie. We don't need makeup," Aileen Death-Banshee said. "And wardrobe? Just look at us, we're in wardrobe! Not that anyone is going to see us anyway."

"We're going to kill Morgan Freeman and nobody will be able to see our grand moment?" Vincent Death decried.

"I'm not Morgan Freeman, I'm God," Morgan Freeman said.

"Well, God, let's see you act your way out of this one," Vincent Death said.

Morgan Freeman turned to the camera. He was dressed in splendid white linens that glowed and made him look ethereal. He gave a very poignant speech, the type of speech that would later garner him his final Academy Award, posthumously of course. When he finished his speech and left the perfect amount of silence for reflection from each and every audience member he winked at the camera. It was the most friendly wink Morgan Freeman had ever mustered up for the camera and everyone watching knew it was going to be alright.

The scene cut from a close up of Morgan Freeman as God and then went to a long shot. Angels heralded just above a triumphant piece of movie score and Morgan Freeman, as God, rose off the set and ascended into a Hollywood set creator's vision of Heaven.

For Morgan Freeman, Vincent Death and Aileen Death-Banshee, it was good enough. Morgan Freeman disappeared off camera and was whisked off to the the River Styx by Vincent Death, and They met Charon on the bank, waiting patiently on his skiff.

"Here is our charge for the day. Morgan Freeman."

"I'm God," Morgan Freeman said.

"He thinks he's God," Vincent Death said to

Charon.

"I am God. I don't think it," Morgan Freeman said.

"They get a little delusional sometimes when you take them to the other side," Aileen Death-Banshee said, apologizing for Morgan Freeman's delusion.

"No, actually, he is not wrong. He is God," Charon said, his voice still gravely but sounding much better now as he continued to suck on a cough drop.

"What?" the Deaths asked in unison.

"It's kinda complicated but, well, just trust me, this is a special delivery."

Morgan Freeman stepped onto Charon's skiff and Charon pushed off.

Morgan Freeman winked at the Deaths, and the skiff disappeared in a flash of white light.

"Well, that was strange," Vincent Death said to Aileen Death-Banshee.

"I'll say. What do you want for dinner tonight?" she asked.

"You," Vincent Death said.

They clasped hands and vanished back along the purple plasma highway. They snuggled the rest of the night and did what Deaths and Death-Banshees do when they are alone in the privacy of their own quarters and under the covers. And since a Death and Death-Banshee had never been together before, they were the only ones who knew the answer to that question.

The End

A Death In Tennessee

A Bonus Short Story

Death sat across from Death at the break room table. Both were sipping on their coffees, preparing to face the day. One of the Death's face was hidden deep within the black hood of his tattered robe, a long white beard cascaded out of the bottom of the black void to indicate there was indeed something in the black void. A smog of fine dust also clung to the air around him.

The death sitting across from him looked like most other Deaths. He was also clothed in a black, tattered robe but his skeletal facial features were easily seen framed within the hood of the robe. Both of their scythes were leaning against the wall of lockers by their table.

"How's it going, Rookie?" Death asked Death over the steaming coffee he was bringing up to his bony mouth.

The Rookie peered into the depths of his own cup of coffee through the black, empty spaces of his eye sockets. He sighed, "Good so far I guess, Old-Timer." came his snooty reply. Though his face was pure bone and no flesh, the bone flexed and moved like rubber as he spoke and made various expressions. This was a quirky physicality of all Deaths.

The old-timer could see he was getting nowhere in breaking the ice with the new guy. He knew he should have sat at the other table with Death. Sure, the Death at that other table smelled kind of funky but when it came down to it, all the Death's smelled kind of funky. It came part and parcel with the job.

"Look, kid" the Old-Timer went on, "I know this gig ain't all you thought it was cracked up to be. You're still wet under the tattered robe, you gotta learn to have fun with this job or you're never going to make your way across the Styx."

The Rookie raised a bony brow at the Old-Timer, he wasn't buying into the spiel. Yet, he hadn't written the old guy off. Instead he sipped on his own coffee waiting for the old-timer to go on with his point.

"I get it. You're guiding souls to the other side. It's a dirty job but someone's gotta do it. You. Me. We're stuck doing it. That's the way it is. So, why not have some fun with it. It's clear the work is getting you down already and that's because you're playing it buy the books.

"You knock on a door, tell 'em its time to go. They beg and plead that you got it all wrong. Just one more day. Cry, cry. Sob, sob. Too bad, so sad."

"Okay, so what's your point?" the Rookie asked.

"You gotta have fun with the job, ya know? Shake things up a little bit. Don't play it buy the book all the time. The supervisors, they aren't always watching. They are barely watching. They're playing Words With Deaths on their iPads."

"What do you mean?"

The Old Timer motioned to a sheet of paper sitting on the table in from on the rookie. "What's on the agenda for today?"

The Rookie, without looking down at the paper, sighed and said, "Chattanooga."

"You see. Right there, that's your problem! I can hear it in your voice. Just another stupid day in stupid Chattanooga with all the big hills and trains and trees and–" The old timer paused and mocked a yawn, "just boring old Chattanooga like the rest of the humdrum state of Tennessee"

"You're trying to tell me there is excitement in collecting souls in Chattanooga?"

"I'm telling you there is excitement in collecting souls everywhere in Tennessee, you just gotta know how!" exclaimed the Old Timer.

The Old Timer scanned over his own work order for the day which was in front of him. He blew off the dust that had settled on it, an unfortunate side effect of being a Death of advanced age, you leave piles of dust all around you.

"I'll tell you what, my work load for the day is pretty easy. I could get a lot of this done later and there are some that can even wait until tomorrow if need be. Why don't I go with you to

Chattanooga and shake things up a bit?"

"Ahhh, Old-Timer, that's real nice of you and all but I don't want to cause any trouble with the higher ups. I just got this gig and I don't want to get fired already. I don't want to get fired at all actually. You and I both know what life is like for an unemployed Death." The Rookie said.

"Baloney! They bosses won't even notice. As long as the work gets done they don't even care! If I do get caught on the job with you I'll just tell them it was an advanced training exercise or something like that. C'mon kid, do this and you will learn to love the job in no time!"

The Rookie looked around the break room. Most of the other Deaths that were sitting around chatting were now up and on their way to their job assignments. The Rookie was eager to get moving himself. He didn't want to be noticed as one of the last ones out the door, He knew he wasn't going to shake the Old Timer off so he agreed to let him come along in haste. He figured he could just shake him off once they were out on assignment.

The Rookie threw back the last of his coffee. It poured down the gap in his skull and spilled out from under his jaw bone and soaked into his tattered black robe. To a human this would look like a big mess but to most Deaths there was no other way to start the day then with a hot cup of joe spilled all over their standard issue tattered robe.

"Well, am I coming with you?" The Old

Timer asked, though he wasn't really giving him an option.

"Yeah, let's go." the Rookie replied.

They made their way out of the break room and on to Chattanooga. The Old Timer left a thick trail of dust in his wake.

Was the Old Timer being poetic? Was he sending them not on a Stairway To Heaven but a Railway To Heaven? The Rookie actually kind of liked that artistic take on it. He eased his concerns about the Old Timer cutting up and getting them in trouble with the bosses. He followed the group on to the train car and found out this was no ordinary train.

"This is the Chattanooga Incline Railway" The Old Timer announced, once the old people and the Rookie were seated, "It is a funicular rail line."

***

The pair materialized on top of an old steam locomotive chugging into Chattanooga. The Old-Timer's long white beard flapped in the breeze, a cloud of dust wisped behind him like a contrail. The Rookie stood next to him struggling to keep the wind from blowing his hood back off his skull.

The steamer pulled into its station and the two Deaths floated down off the top of the train. There was a bevvy of action on the platform below; people exiting and entering the train all around. None took notice of the Deaths at all.

People never really noticed Death until Death came knocking at their doors.

"Okay, how many do we have in Chattanooga?" the Old-Timer asked.

The Rookie scanned his work assignment, "Twelve." he replied, "And I'm not wasting any more time with train rides. That served no purpose, riding on that old steam engine like we're some kind of tourists."

The Old-Timer squealed in laughter. "Son, you haven't been to Chattanooga until you've rode the old historic railroad. Now you can say you've been to Chattanooga for real!"

The Rookie just shook his head and headed for their first destination. There was an old folks home just up the street from the Train Museum they just wasted their time at. The Chattanooga job would be simple. All twelve of his pick-ups in the city were located at the elderly home.

The Rookie made his rounds once he got there. Collecting the souls at an old age home was often a hassle-free experience. The souls were either eager to finally go somewhere or were delusional enough to believe The Rookie was their cousin Mel come to visit from Miami.

"Okay, let's get these folks on the skiff to there hereafter so we can move on to our next job." the Rookie announced once he had the pick-ups all together.

"Whoa, whoa, whoa! Easy cowboy. Lesson

one: The job is done, now have some fun." the Old-Timer said.

"What's that supposed to mean? The job isn't done. We have to get them to the skiff for the ride across the Styx."

The Old-Timer waved him off, "You're playing it by the book. The job only states we have to get them to the Hereafter. The Book doesn't specify that we have do it via Charon and his silly little boat now does it?"

"Well, no" The Rookie said considering the exact wording of the policy book, "but that's how we were trained so..."

"So what? I have a much more memorable way to send these fine folks off to their new lives. Follow me!"

The Old-Timer marched off and the Rookie's charges followed him like he was some kind of tour guide and they were finally off to do something other than bingo and crocheting in the main dining hall.

The Rookie sighed and ran after them to catch up.

They arrived at the Chattanooga Incline Railway. The Rookie had no idea why the Old Timer had brought them here but he began to postulate a theory in his hollow skull when he surveyed the scene. There was a quaint little railway station situation at the bottom of a Mount Lookout as all the signs around had dubbed it.

There were two sets of railroad tracks that exited the station and cut their way up the side of the mountain. It looked like a steep climb.

"Did you say a funicular? What the heck is a funicular?" The Rookie asked.

"I'm glad you asked," the Old Timer said acting like some sort of tour guide, "A funicular is a unique type of rail road. It uses twin rail cars and a cable system to scale the side of steep hill and mountains. One car counterweights the other car to assist in the fight of gravity. As one car goes up the mountain, its sister car descends via the cable. It's a simple, elegant and rather amusing way to traverse the side of a mountain.

"Like this mountain. Mount Lookout, famous for Rock City at the top. The mountain actually straddles the border between Tennessee and Georgia. So if you'll all stay seated and keep your arms and feet inside the vehicle at all times, we will begin our journey to your final destination."

The old people all applauded. They were delighted to be out and on a free sightseeing trip. The Rookie got up and sat next to the Old Timer at the head of the train car as it pulled out of the station and began its ascent to the top of Lookout Mountain.

"So this isn't some sort of poetic end to their lives? No great climb to Heaven? We're just out sight seeing?"

"Watch and learn," was all the Old Timer said as he looked out the window and enjoyed the scenery as the peculiar train wandered its way up the mountain side.

The funicular labored the last few inches into the station at the top of Lookout Mountain. Before it could line up with the station platform to allow everyone to disembark, the Old Timer stood up and assumed his tour guide position once again.

"Ladies and Gentlemen, please remain seated until the train has come to a full and complete stop. This concludes your journey here with us. Have a pleasant afterlife."

The Old Timer picked up his scythe and walked out the front of the train onto the open air deck just at the front of the car. The Rookie didn't know if he should follow directions and stay seated with the rest of them or if he was supposed to go with the Old Timer for a bit more of his unorthodox training regimen. After a moments debate he hopped up and joined the Old Timer out on the front of the train.

The Rookie walked out the front of the car just in time to see the Old Timer leaning over the front rail of the train car. The Rookie would have feared the Old Timer was leaning over so far that he might fall and die but the Old Timer was technically already dead.

And then the Rookie saw him do something worse. The Old Timer's arm swung back behind him, scythe in hand. His arm swung back down toward the tracks, the blade of the scythe a silver streak blur.

The sound that followed was like the world's largest out of tune guitar string being plucked. A miserable TWANG split the air and before The Rookie could register what had happened, the train began to roll backwards.

The Old Timer faded out of existence as the funicular car raced free of its cable down one of the steepest grades any train in the world climbed. It didn't take long for the train car to build up tremendous amount of speed. It was good fortune that most of the seniors on board were experiencing some level of dementia and did not fully grasp the gravity of their situation. One old man even had his hands in the air screaming, "Wheeeeeeeeee!"

Rookie had no idea what he was going to do. Was he supposed to save them now? What is the point of saving the lives of souls he's supposed to deliver to the other side anyway? None of this made sense! He had no clue what the Old Timer wanted him to do. Time was running out as the train was now rocketing at over one hundred miles an hour down the side of Lookout Mountain.

"Wheeeeeeeee heeee heee heeeeee!"

The Rookie heard the jubilation and looked up at the roof of the railcar. He shook his head, vanished then rematerialized on top of the runaway train. Sure enough, the Old Timer was standing on top of the train riding it like it was a surfboard and he was Michael J. Fox in Teen Wolf.

"Are you kidding me right now?" The Rookie yelled over the thunder of the air rushing by them.

"Oh grow up!" The Old Timer waved him off, dismissive of his concerns. He lifted one leg under his tattered robe, hot dogging down the mountain.

"So this is it? This is your big plan? Get them all killed before they can get to the other side? This is what you just had to show me? Committing career suicide is how I'm supposed to have fun with the job?" The Rookie said, irritated that he agreed to any of this.

"No, we're killing them so they can get to the other side. Look, it doesn't matter how they get there, just that they get there. We are only guides. We have to show them the way. Just because there is a boat that takes them there all nice and neat doesn't mean we have to use that method. We can do whatever we want as long as our charges end up on the other side."

The Rookie stared at the Old Timer through his empty eye sockets, dumbfounded. The grade began to flatten out as the car raced at over two hundred miles per hour and neared the station at the bottom. Gravity and inertia began to push the two Deaths down on the roof.

"Now, surf this bitch while you have a few

seconds and then let's split. It's almost the end of the line." the Old Timer said.

The Rookie didn't surf, he wasn't getting it. Instead both Death's leapt off into the ether just before the train slammed into the station at the bottom of Lookout Mountain in Chattanooga, Tennessee. The papers reported the "untimely" passing of the twelve elderly people on board who had apparently suffered from a rare case of mass dementia and had gone joy riding on the train in the middle of the night. The youngest of them was ninety two.

A local official quoted it as a terrible accident that took the lives of so many people with so much potential.

***

"Where to next?" the Old Timer asked the Rookie as they floated through the vortex of time and space that Death's use to get from here to there.

"Where to? I'll tell you where to! We're headed right back to headquarters because I'm turning your crazy ass in! That's where to!" The Rookie yelled. It was a good thing he had no skin covering his skull or he'd be flush red.

"Okay! Okay! Look, I get it. I sprung that on you. You weren't ready for that much excitement all at once. I swear, I'll take it down a few notches. Give me one more shot. We'll still have all the fun without all the blood and gore this time. Please."

The Rookie would have rolled his eyeballs if he had any.

"Pigeon Falls. And this is it. I don't care if it goes better here. This is the last assignment you're coming along for. I'm not cut out for your kind of fun ."

"Fair enough Rookie. Let's go."

The two Death's arrived in a dense forested area. The Rookie was worried there was a forest fire nearby and that they had the unfortunate chore of leading charred bodies away from their dooms and on to their eternal afterlives.

The Old Timer snickered in a high pitched choke at the Rookie when he pulled his tattered robe up over his mouth and nose cavities to filter what he thought was thick smoke.

"You dope. We're in the Smoky Mountains. There ain't no fire. Its dense fog, it's always like this in this part of Tennessee. Now who's on the roster here?" the Old Timer asked looking over the Rookie's shoulder at his manifest.

Before the Rookie could utter the words, the Old Timer cut him off, "You've got to be shitting me. They assigned you to her?"

The Old Timer was carrying on about Rookie's new assignment. Rookie had no idea what the big deal was, a soul was a soul was a soul. He began to get the idea when they arrived at their destination. A grand cabin situated well away from the rest of the world in the middle of these smoky mountains.

The Rookie rang the doorbell. It sounded off with a melody that was somehow familiar to him. A song he could name on the tip of his tongue but not quite get off. It sounded country and popish and very eighties.

The door opened and a buxom blonde stood on the other side of the threshold.

"It's you!" The Old Timer said, star-struck.

"It's you!" the blonde said, frightened.

The Rookie still had no idea who this woman was. She was blonde but it was definitely a wig. She was old but still smoking hot, she could have been thirty or she could have been eighty. It was hard to gauge. However, her most striking feature were her ample breasts. Wow, what a bust!

The Old Timer extended his bony arm to the blonde. A plume of dust exploded from around it.

"Dolly Parton. Gosh! I'm such a big fan. This is a real treat."

"I wish i could say the same!" Dolly Parton said in her big honking southern drawl.

The Rookie interceded the star gazing moment, "Yeah, well, it is what it is and we have to get going. You're not the only one on the list today, so if you'll just come with us—"

"No way," Old Timer protested. "You can't take Dolly Parton! Look at her! She's still hot, she's still got it! Those breasts ain't ready to die! She's a class act."

"Come on Old Timer," the Rookie said exasperated, "you promised you wouldn't cut up this time. Let's just do what we came to do and get this day over with already."

"No. I won't let you take Dolly Parton. Did you hear that doorbell? Nine to Five!"

"What does a doorbell have to do with anything? It's her time to go. It's right on the paper in black ink. It's her time. Let's go."

The Old Timer stepped in between Dolly Parton and The Rookie and folded his arms across his emaciated chest. Dolly Parton was engulfed in a cloud of the Old Timer's dust.

"Look," Dolly Parton said, swatting away the dusty cloud, "I think the other guy is right. It is my time. I understand and accept that somehow. But if I'm going out, I'm going out with a bang. Ya'll wait right here while I put on my southern best. And, if you don't mind, there's somewhere I'd like to see one last time before we go."

"That'll be just fine Ms. Parton." The Rookie said, only he looked directly at the Old Timer giving him the 'I-told-you-so' look. After Dolly closed the door to get changed, the Rookie looked the Old Timer dead in the eye socket, "She's a class act."

"You're not taking her." the Old Timer said like a five year old brat not getting his way.

"I am taking her. That's the job." the Rookie said like his five year old mother who wasn't going to budge.

Before Old Timer had a chance to clock the Rookie over the head, Dolly Parton was back at the door, dressed to the nines in a tight fitting, sparkling, rhinestone dress. He ample bosoms now appeared to defy gravity and the laws of physics with the space they were able to occupy. It was a lot of mass in a little bit of space.

Dolly requested that before it was her time to cross over to the other side she wanted to visit her favorite place in the whole wide world one more time. Dollywood. Each Death placed a hand on Dolly Parton and the disappeared from the front of her sprawling, rural estate and reappeared among the mayhem of a very busy afternoon in Dollywood.

There we families everywhere. Children squealed with delight. Adults smiled watching their family enjoying a carefree day. They were all having too much fun to notice the park's namesake and her two grim reaper friends appear out of thin air.

"Boys, I just love me some roller coasters. I made sure to have the best roller coasters right here in Dollywood. So as my final request, I'd like to ride my favorite roller coasters here in Dollywood one last time. Is that okay with all ya'll?" Dolly Parton asked.

"That sounds like fun Ms. Parton. We can

ride all day and all night long if you'd like." The Old Timer said from somewhere deep within his tattered hooded robe. He was trying to buy Dolly Parton some time until he could figure a way to rescue her from the Rookie.

"Absolutely!" The Rookie with jubilance the Old Timer found just a bit disturbing.

"Great! Let's go on the Runaway train ride I just had put in. It's a blast, ya'll are gonna love it to pieces!" she said and stomped her rhinestone boot and pinched the bone of the Rookie's skeletal cheek.

The Old Timer made the Rookie hang back a few paces behind Dolly. Dolly was too boisterous and full of energy to notice they were lagging. When Old Timer was confident they were out of earshot, he picked up his argument again.

"Look at her, she's much too peppy for a person whose time has come. Someone back at the office has made a mistake."

"You know the office never makes a mistake. Never. You can't stop this. I have a job to do and I intend to do it." The Rookie replied.

They approached the line for the runaway train roller coaster. They took up position next to Dolly as she marveled at the ride from the barrier fencing.

"You know, Ms Parton, my colleague here was just showing me how much fun trains can be just this morning." Rookie said in as pleasant a tone as he could muster.

"No." Old Timer whispered under his breath.

"Oh I just love trains too," Dolly said, "there's just something so southern about them." She took the Old Timer by the arm, "And I just love a man who loves trains. C'mon you're riding up front with me, sugar!"

Being Dolly in Dollywood has its perks. They were able to cut right to the front of the line and have their pick of which seat on the roller coaster they wanted. The Old Timer scrunched up as close to Dolly Parton as he could. To most people it would have looked like the Old Timer was a hopeless romantic his girlfriend on the roller coaster she was only pretending to be scared of. The Rookie knew otherwise, he knew the Old Timer was protect Dolly Parton from her own death. He smiled. Payback is a bitch.

The runaway train rolled gently out of the station and latched on the chain lift. The coaster crept up the first hill with the signature *clack-clack-clack-clack-clack* of the chain rattling underneath. The Rookie crooked a finger at the lap bar holding Dolly and the Old Timer in the train car. It rose off their laps and the Old Timer slammed it down just as quick as it rose. He stifled a nervous laugh and was thankful

The train crested the first hill and they were off. It swooped down blowing Dolly Parton's wig back but it never fell out of place. The Old Timer left a trail of dust behind him that blew right into the Rookie's face. He wasn't bothered as he spent the entire ride trying to unlatch the restraining device. The Old Timer wasn't having as much fun as Dolly Parton because he had to spend the entire ride holding her in the train. She only thought he was being a little scaredy cat.

"Woo hoo! Let's go on one of the BIG ones!" Dolly Parton thundered in her big southern belle voice after they exited the runaway train unscathed. She grabbed the Rookie around the waist, "This time you're riding with me sugar pie!"

"Oh no." the Old Timer said, dejected.

Dolly Parton led them to a very intimidating looking roller coaster called The Wild Eagle. She told them it was the first winged rollercoaster built in the U.S, She was very proud of this fact and she beamed at it like she was looking a grand old American flag. The seats on the cars for this roller coaster were situated in a way that they sat even with the tracks. Thus, the roller coaster train resembled a winged creature. The benefit was in the twists and turns this coaster was able to pull off. It was an engineering marvel and the worst nightmare of a person with a weak constitution.

They were able to once again bypass the long lines. The Rookie rode up front next to Dolly this time while the Old Timer was now relegate to the bitch seat just behind them. The train rolled out of the station and clanked up the lift hill. The Rookie wasted no time in making this as perilous a ride for

Dolly Parton as he could. The Old Timer heard the over-the-shoulder restraint unlock as soon as the coaster began to climb the hill. He reached over with his scythe and pushed the restraint back down.

The coaster dove down the first hill and banked hard to the right. The Rookie unlocked the seat restraint once more. Dolly Parton was almost flung from the train but the Old Timer was dead set on keeping her alive. He disappeared from his seat and rematerialized right on top of Dolly Parton's harness, locking it back in place before the laws of physics could put an end to her life.

"I'm not letting you do this! Not today!" The Old Timer yelled over the sound of rolling thunder the roller coaster produced.

"What's the matter? Can't take a dose of your own medicine? I'm just having fun, just like you showed me!" The Rookie yelled back.

"Boys! Boys! Just what in tarnation are y'all doing?" Dolly Parton cried out, arms still waving in the air as she enjoyed the ride despite the annoyance of her new companions.

The Deaths didn't hear Dolly. The Rookie jabbed his scythe at the Old Timer to knock him off balance. The Old Timer parried and countered with a thrust of his own scythe. The Rookie ducked down as the blade arced over his head. The both swung at the same time and the blades of their scythes sparked against the other, It was just like the final duel between Darth Vader and Obi

Wan Kenobi. Except, Dolly Parton was not the pansy farm boy that Luke was.

She reached up and pulled both Deaths down as the roller coaster went through a long down sweeping curl. "Why are you two fighting on my ride?" she demanded.

"He's trying to kill you." The Old Timer said matter-of-fact.

"It's true." The Rookie said.

"Well, I know that! That's what this is all about isn't it? Isn't this my chance to go out how I choose?"

"Well, yes Ms. Parton," The Old Timer said, now as bashful as a kid with his hand caught in the cookie jar, "but you're a legend."

"You can't be a legend until you're dead. That's a fact,. Knock it off and let me go then sugar." Dolly said.

She tugged the Old Timer by the neck of his robe. She pulled the dark empty space inside his hood down into her breasts and let him have a good snogging in Dolly's own Great Smoky Mountains. The Old Timer cam up swooning, dust swirling all around his head.

The Rookie flicked a bony finger at the restraining device. The lap bar rose up just as the roller coaster crested the final hill. The laws of physics threw Dolly Parton from the roller coaster and she splattered into the mock up of an old mine shack the coaster dove under just before entering the station. Dolly Parton was a bloody, splattered mess on the side of the old, splintered building.

"Hmph," The Old Timer observed, "I guess they are real. I was expecting to see two silicone implants bounce off her remains. What a woman."

"Now we're even." The Rookie said.

"And," The Old Timer added, "you had fun. Didn't you?"

"Son of a bitch, you tricked me didn't you?"

The Old Timer shrugged. The Rookie couldn't see his skeletal expression but he would have gambled there was a coy smile on the Old Timer's face at that moment. Still, The Rookie did have to admit, there was a certain satisfaction he got out of the Dolly Parton job. In fact, he felt rejuvenated and reenergized. There was still one more job on the manifest and he had to admit, he felt ready to get at it.

"You seem to have a little extra pep in your step now, Rookie. I'm glad to see you finally had some fun with the job. Anyway, I promised I would leave you alone after this one so I guess I'll get going to cover my assignments for the day. I might have enough time to cover them all being as its still so early yet." The Old Timer offered the Rookie his dusty hand.

"Wait," The Rookie hesitated, calculating his words, "I hate to admit it but you were right. This horsing around on the job thing isn't so bad after all. For the first time I don't feel like a cog in the system. I feel like I own this job, like I was born to do this—"

"You were born to do this." The Old Timer said, pointing out the obvious.

"I now. That's not what I meant. What I mean is that I feel like this is what I should be doing. I feel like I want to get right to the next assignment. I feel like I can't wait to go home and wake up the next morning and get at it again!"

"Atta boy. Well, I'll be off now. Catch you around." The Old Timer waved and began to fade out of sight.

"Hold on! Do you want to come on my last assignment for the day?" The Rookie asked. He looked down at his manifest and grinned, "It's going to be a doozy!"

"Woo Hoo!" The Old Timer faded back into existence, "I thought you'd never ask! What do we got next?"

"How's your singing voice?" The Rookie asked.

***

Death looked at Death.

"Are you ready?" The Rookie asked the Old Timer.

"I look ridiculous."

"Now, who's the one not having any fun?"

[176]

The Rookie chided.

"Shut up." Was all the Old Timer had in him for a reply.

"Oh, knock it off. You look fine. They are going to love you!"

The Old Timer tried to adjust the Stetson adorned upon his head. It just felt weird wearing a Stetson over the top of the hood of his tattered robe. The big cowboy boots he was wearing were too new and too stiff for a Death that was used to going barefoot everywhere. And the coup de grace was the big steel guitar he was holding felt big and clunky as opposed to his normally thin and nimble scythe.

"So, who is this friend of yours that you called in for the job?" The Old Timer asked, trying to take his mind of the country western singer gear.

"You'll see, she'll be here soon. Look alive though, it's almost time for us to go on."

Butterflies took flight in the hollow chest cavity of The Old Timer's dusty rib cage. Moths he was used to flying around inside him, but not butterflies. The Rookie was really taking this fun thing to a new level. He'd created a monster.

The house lights dimmed and applause from the other side of the curtain exploded. The hum of amplifiers grew and vibrated the stage. A godlike voice from overhead announced the band about to take the stage.

"It's Grand Ole Opry time!" hollered a voice with a classic southern twang.

The curtains rose and both Death's were bathed in spotlights as they walked forward playing a country ditty that had the crowd on their feet at the first strains. They approached their microphones, the Rookie's at stage right and the Old Timer's at stage left.

They began to sing a song that sounded something like Hank Williams Jr. and Rob Zombie collaborated on. It was eerie and catchy at the same time. The crowd began to clap along. The Death's were basking in the moment.

The song bridged into the chorus, the guitars rising to a crescendo. A blast of brilliant white light burst from just above center stage. The audience cowered from the blast of light and then leered in as the light softened and reveal a specter-like woman draped in a tattered, flowing black robe similar but more feminine than the grim reapers wore. She was a Banshee.

The Banshee flittered down to the stage from where she levitated at catwalk level. She hovered over the the microphone at center stage and began to wail the chorus of the song. The sound was majestic and horrific at the same time. The crowd didn't know if they should run or swoon. Even the Old Timer and the Rookie seemed confused as to join in the chorus or run away from the beautifully awful wailing.

In the end, there wasn't enough time to make

a decision. Everyone who was exposed to the sound of the Banshee's wail was dead where they stood in the Grand Ole Opry auditorium. When the final body dropped, the Banshee ceased her wailing and floated off into the ether.

The Rookie and Old Timer stopped playing. Their assignments were now completed for the day.

***

The next morning...

Death sat across from Death at the break room table. Death sipped his coffee as if he had already had a cup this morning, but he hadn't. The Rookie had a pep to him that he hadn't had before. The Old Timer sipped his own coffee, smiling inside his blackened chest, knowing this rookie Death was now on board with the program. He would be sticking around for sure.

"I had a lot of fun yesterday. I didn't think the job could be that enjoyable in a million years. The last bit was just the icing on the cake." The Rookie said as coffee began to soak the chest of his tattered black robe.

"Yeah, I mean it was a bitch dragging all those bodies over to The Styx but the look on Charon's face when we piled the bodies up on his skiff and nearly sank it was priceless!" The Old Timer hooted.

"I know you have to play catch up with your

own assignments now Old Timer, but whenever you're having a slow day you are more than welcome to come along with me again. That was a blast. Thank you for opening my eyes, I learned a lot."

"I have to admit," The Old Timer said, "that bit about bringing the Banshee in to polish off all those people in The Grand Ole Opry was nothing short of brilliant."

The Rookie paused mid-sip of coffee, pulling it back from his jaw. "Huh? I didn't call in the Banshee." he said, confused.

"But you said you were going to call in a friend." the Old Timer said, now confused himself.

"Yeah, Loretta Lynn. But she canceled. I didn't want to tell you in case you freaked out. I just figured you called in the Banshee. You seem to be that kind of crazy."

"Wasn't me." replied the Old Timer.

The two Deaths fell deep into contemplation. If neither of them had called in the Banshee, it could mean big trouble. Banshee's knew their place and dared not encroach on Grim Reaper territories. If that Banshee showed up and took a job from them, the ramifications could be dire.

The great power struggle between Deaths and Banshees may well have just begun.

Frank J. Edler resides in New Jersey, a land of the weird and unnatural. He is the author of the short story collection, *Scared Silly and* co-author of the horror humor series, *Shocker.* His short stories have been published in various anthologies including *Strange Versus Lovecraft, Strange Fucking Stories, Still Dying 2* as well as several volumes of the *State of Horror* anthology series. Frank is also clandestinely known as Mr. Frank, host the wildly popular Bizzong! Podcast on Project iRadio and co-host of the irreverent podcast *Books, Beer and Bullshit.*

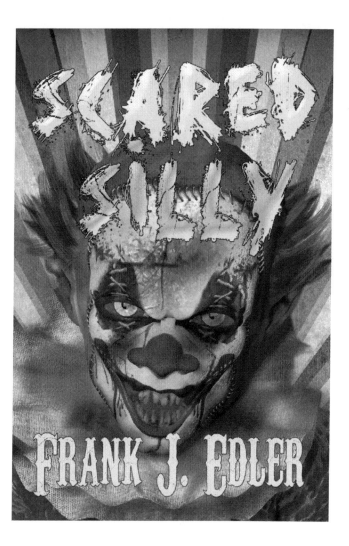

28412093R00117

Made in the USA
Columbia, SC
10 October 2018